High Praise for

Tink and Wendy

by Kelly Ann Jacobson

30 MUST-READ QUEER fairytale retellings for pride!

BOOK RIOT

BEST LGBTQA+ BOOKS of 2021!

SHE READS

A MASTERFUL REINVENTION of the classic. Full of teenage angst and yearning, it is poignant, relatable, and full of contemporary appeal.

FOREWORD REVIEWS

A CHARACTER-DRIVEN REIMAGINING of *Peter Pan* . . . a queer, introspective retelling.

KIRKUS REVIEWS

MADE ME FEEL the same way I felt when I was little reading the original Peter Pan stories, that sense of something magical, just right out of your reach. Like magic was really possible. . . . 5 stars, more if it was possible.

MY CAT READS AND REVIEWS

HEADSTRONG, CLEVER, AND haunted by her past, Jacobson's Tink is the Jessica Jones of Neverland—even sharing her appreciation for a good, stiff drink. But make no mistake, this Tink is very much her own unique character, navigating complex relationships with Peter and Wendy. Jacobson breathes new life into traditional Peter Pan lore, shuttling her protagonists between modern-day upstate New York and a Neverland built and managed by fairies. *Tink and Wendy* is a delight for fans of *Peter Pan*, but easily has the richness and heart to stand on its own.

TARA CAMPBELL, Author, *Cabinet of Wrath: A Doll Collection*

QUEER READERS SUCH as myself who spent their childhoods escaping into the fantastical worlds of Oz and Neverland will delight in Kelly Ann Jacobson's *Tink and Wendy*. Witty, gritty, and magical, Tink and Wendy is an homage to J.M. Barrie's imagination even as it flips his script. News flash: It's not all about the boys anymore!

JULIA WATTS, Author, *Quiver* and *Needlework*

TINK AND WENDY isn't simply a brilliant, queer revision; it's *Peter Pan* as I wish it had always been. Readers will adore Tink's candor and her journey through grief, devotion, and redemption. This legend is enriched by Kelly Ann Jacobson's talent and wit. *Tink and Wendy* joins the ranks of *Boy, Snow, Bird* by Helen Oyeyemi, *The Robber Bride* by Margaret Atwood, and *The Color Master: Stories* by Aimee Bender and will become the classic that replaces the classic.

MELISSA SCHOLES YOUNG, Author, *The Hive* and *Flood*

AS A CHILD, I was fascinated with J.M. Barrie's Peter Pan, but just like Mary Shelley's Victor Frankenstein, quickly grew weary of the singular focus on the privileged, overly entitled boy who never grew up, but somehow ends up with the most self-sacrificing and parentified girl-child of classic young adult literature. Jacobson's *Tink and Wendy* offers the retelling I've always dreamed of—one that masterfully builds layers upon layers, at long last, to these two complex characters, each on the opposite end of the same coin, while staying true to the recognizable characteristics of Barrie's original. Jacobson has created a formidable and necessary addition to the Peter Pan mythology, one that refreshingly centers the complexities of motherhood and womanly expectations of hyperresponsibility via a queer looking glass. A must read for any fan of the Peter Pan canon.

ADDIE TSAI, Author, *Dear Twin*

Tink and Wendy

Tink and Wendy

a novel

Kelly Ann Jacobson

THREE ROOMS PRESS
New York, NY

Tink and Wendy
A Novel by Kelly Ann Jacobson

ISBN 978-1-953103-13-0 (trade paperback)
ISBN 978-1-953103-14-7 (Epub)
Library of Congress Control Number: 2021935384

TRP-093

First Edition
Pub Date: October 26, 2021

Young Adult Fiction: Ages 14 and up
BISAC Coding:
YAF031000 Young Adult Fiction / LGBT
YAF037000 Young Adult Fiction / Loners & Outcasts
YAF058120 Young Adult Fiction / Social Themes / Friendship
YAF058260 Young Adult Fiction / Social Themes / Values & Virtues

COVER DESIGN AND ILLUSTRATION:
Victoria Black: www.thevictoriablack.com

BOOK DESIGN:
KG Design International: www.katgeorges.com

DISTRIBUTED IN THE U.S. AND INTERNATIONALLY BY:
Publishers Group West www.pgw.com

Three Rooms Press
New York, NY
www.threeroomspress.com
info@threeroomspress.com

For Zoe and Lyla

Tink and Wendy

PART ONE

CHAPTER ONE

"Introduction"

Excerpt from *Neverland: A History*

Not many people know this, but the fairies were the ones who created Neverland in the first place. Before they planted the seed of the first Never tree in Neverland's fertile ground, that starfish-shaped rock had been just that: a rock where pirates on their way to better lands docked for a few days to stretch their legs, or to bury their treasures in the lagoon where many years later mermaids would find the gold coins and use them as decorations for their hair. This was a hundred years before anyone had heard of Peter Pan, or the Lost Boys, or Wendy, or even Tinker Bell.

That last name, I must pause to acknowledge, is the reason I have been tasked with the honor of writing this volume, the first-ever history of what has become quite a legendary land. I was Tink's superior officer at the time of her assignment to watch over Peter Pan, and in fact it was I who selected her from the dozens of new recruits who needed posts.

Why, you might ask, did I choose such a strong-willed, anti-authoritarian, at times even ill-mannered fairy for such an important task?

Obviously, you never met Peter.

CHAPTER TWO

Now

TINK WAKES EARLY, AT THE TIME when the sun blinks through the trunks of the elms around her cottage and through the missing pane of her front window, and then turns her back on the new day. The sun, like a dog, chases her over the wool blanket, against the wall, into the bed, until she has no choice but to push off her covers and meet the morning.

The wood floor is cold against her bare feet. The water in her basin is cold, though she splashes her face anyway and wipes herself on a grimy hand towel on the table. The fabric of her army jacket is cold until the heat of her body warms it.

Everything is cold in upstate New York.

There might be more snow later, though Tink doesn't have that special itch in her nose that precipitates a storm. Her breath hangs in front of her as a brief specter, then disappears, leaving her gaunt face in the mirror. She looks hungover. She is hungover. The bottle of wine she stole from the bar in town lies empty on its side, a dribble of red liquid now stained on the wooden table. They know her by name; they have her picture hung up next to the cash register. UNDERAGE: DO NOT SERVE.

Tink smears her short blonde hair back and it stays that way, slick with grease. She zippers up the jacket. Her eyes are bloodshot and fearless, like a rabid animal's. Her skin is dull. Once, a long time ago, she was beautiful, but those days are long gone—or, rather, she has banished them. Beauty has never brought her anything, and she's tired of expecting otherwise.

After she turns away from the mirror, she slides on her boots and takes up her bucket filled with tools: soft bristle brush, wood scraper, sponge, and a piece of flannel ripped from an old shirt. She rips a chunk from a loaf of stale bread, finds the butter in the fridge, and slides the rough edge of the bread over the butter slab. When she bites into it, crumbs scatter on the floor. Her thermos is waiting on the counter, and she fills it with the coffee from her automatic machine and screws on the lid. Later, the heat from the liquid will bring her some comfort.

When she steps outside, snow slides off of the roof onto her head. She shakes off the flakes, though a few have already melted onto her head, and then slips her jacket's hood up. Her boots crunch footprints into the snow where she walked the night before, the steps going in the opposite direction longer and heavier and more prone to spills on the slippery stones beneath. She doesn't remember walking back from the bar, but the steps are inarguably hers—no one else in town has such small feet.

If she thinks very hard, she can remember the perfect eighty-degree days of Neverland. The slight mist in the air from the lagoon. In the distance, the sound of boys calling out, mostly for Peter. The breeze would tickle her wings and send a chill of anticipation down her spine, for whenever there was a breeze, Peter would come knocking at her door. *Tink, it's flying weather,* he would say, and she would drop whatever she was doing to pass the time between his visits and dive out to meet him. *It's flying weather,* but also cross-the-ocean weather, into-the-window-of-an-unsuspecting-child weather, meeting-Wendy weather. Weather that seemed temperate at the time, though when Tink looks back, there were storms on the horizon.

But to fly . . . to have the wind lift you up by your wings and carry you, to have everything you know grow small, the way a day grows small to someone as stuck in time as she and Peter. What was a single day among so many wonderful days?

It's flying weather.

Tink crosses her yard to the wrought iron fence and opens the gate with her elbow. Still, the cold metal finds its way through the fabric of her jacket, and she shivers. The tools in her basket chatter like teeth. Once she rushes through, the gate creaks closed behind her, like the closing of a book, like the end of a life—not that an immortal fairy like Tink would know about that.

The path that leads from Tink's cottage to the main road is perilous—not just slippery, but also steep and sewn with knotted roots. She trips a few times on the way up, and has to grab a branch here and there with her free hand to remain upright. A rabbit, gray the way the snow will turn after she has walked this path a few times, hops from the bramble and then back in again. This will likely be the only life Tink sees all day.

When she gets to the main road, which is really an unused dirt road that she shares with the few other inhabitants of these woods, she hurries on her way so she won't risk running into one of her well-meaning neighbors. A hundred feet away she turns sharply left again and through another iron gate, this one adorned by a pattern of roses. Three markers forward, two to the left, another three, and there they are, two headstones between the evergreens on the border of the cemetery, only inches apart and marked with identical swans. *What's all the fuss about?* Tink thought when she first saw them—after all, when you have your own wings, there isn't anything special about a clumsy white bird swimming around a lake half the time—but Peter had always admired them. *Do you know they mate for life?* he'd said, and Tink had turned her nose up at the prospect. They were, after all, back in Neverland, where the closest anyone came to "mating for life" was a Lost Boy writing a love letter to one of the mermaids. *Wanna go to the bonfire with me tonight? Circle yes/no.*

She had turned her nose up, and yet far below the surface something had stirred in her, like a fish so far down in the lagoon that it was a mere shadow just barely visible from Marooners' Rock. Something . . . older. This was no child's crush, and yet they were children, she and Peter, or at least that's how they appeared and how they acted and what they told themselves they were. Never growing up.

And yet . . .

She began to notice things about Peter. His long, gangly legs. The strong hands used to slick the fairy dust from her skin. The way he looked when he was thinking happy thoughts, like ice cream and puppies and rainbows filling the sky. She wanted him to look that way at her, but he only ever teased her, his silly fairy girl.

It's flying weather, he said, and she had said *Oh, how I love to fly!* but what she'd meant was, *Oh, I love you Peter.* A man would have understood, but Peter was no man—not then.

Tink ends her journey at the twin headstones. There are no years listed on one; the other, inscribed Wendy Darling, marks her as the youngest of all those buried in the cemetery. Tink kneels and cleans out some moss growing in the number eight, then wipes the snow and dirt from the top of the stone with the soft flannel shirt piece until it shines. Wendy would have done a better job, Tink thinks, and then she wipes the stone a second time for good measure. Once Wendy's stone looks presentable, Tink moves to the second stone, but like always, she cannot bring herself to touch even the top of it with her swatch.

"Damn you," she mutters.

In the trees, birds wake at the sound of her voice and throw themselves into the wind. They'll be back to roost, Tink knows, the way that she and Peter always went back to Neverland, until the night they didn't.

"Damn you," she says again. "Why couldn't you just go home, the way you always did?"

But she's talking to empty air. The birds aren't there, and Peter certainly isn't there.

And why isn't he here, Tink?

She drops the flannel piece in the snow and doesn't pick it up again.

"Because Peter is dead."

CHAPTER THREE

Then

TINKER BELL AND PETER HAD SEVERAL favorite haunts, one of them being Big Ben, which they visited first that fateful night, and another right across the ocean at Niagara Falls. It was actually Tinker Bell who chose their destination—she loved the way the green water, tinted by the tiny rocks ground from the bed of the Niagara River, forced itself forward like a horse that was its own master.

"Watch this!" Peter called from behind the falls. Tink could barely make him out, illuminated though he was in the glow of her fairy dust, until with a surge of force he pounded through the largest portion of water, Horseshoe Falls, and did a series of front flips to where she hovered. Tink put out her arms, always ready to catch him should he lose control, but Peter stopped inches from her face and gave her a beaming smile.

"Silly Peter," Tink said, but she couldn't help smiling back.

"I am silly," he admitted. He ran a hand through his short red hair and then replaced his green cap. "But that's what you like about me, isn't it?"

"Of course it is."

"Good. Because I have a surprise for you," Peter said. Then he wrung his wet cap over her head.

Tink tried to swat the hat away, but Peter was too quick for her. She chased him into the water, out of the water, the force of the falls like a giant hand trying to squash her every time she moved through it, until they were both tired and panting and sweating, though you couldn't tell because they were so wet.

"Let's take a break," said Peter, and he flew back through the falls to their secret cave.

Tink followed, landing on a rock that served as their only chair like a butterfly alighting on the petal of a flower. Peter shook his head like a dog, and Tink spun so that droplets flung from her skirt onto the walls of the cave. After they were as dry as they could be sitting in a damp cave, the two friends sat down on the rock and shared a bar of chocolate Peter had kept safe in a plastic bag in his pocket. All residents of Neverland loved chocolate, but none more than Peter, and whenever he and Tink left home, they always raided a different candy store in order to replenish their stash.

"Better than sleeping in all day," Peter said as he chowed down on a second chunk.

"Better than swimming in the lagoon on a warm afternoon," Tink said. She closed her eyes and let her piece melt on her tongue.

"Better than Christmas morning," Peter said.

"Better than a mother's kiss," Tink said.

No one said anything for a long time after that. Neither Peter nor Tink had a mother—or rather, Tink didn't have a mother, and Peter had never known his—and yet they both yearned for the feeling of a mother's arms the way someone who has never seen the ocean yearns to put their feet in the lapping waves.

"We should get going," Peter said, and Tink agreed, though there was no schedule to their wanderings. They came and went as they pleased, staying in one place only long enough for Tink to replenish her dust or Peter to direct the Lost Boys on a project they should finish before he returned. This time, they were hard at work making arrows Peter could lace with a sleeping potion, should Captain Hook and his dreaded crew sail back to Neverland.

Now, when Tink thinks back to the moment when she pushed back through the falls into the cool fall air, she wonders how different things would have been if she had just aimed a little more to the left, or to the right, or up, or anywhere but directly ahead, where, unbeknownst to the two beings eating chocolate in the cave, a helicopter had stopped to shine a light on the water below. A man had thrown himself into the falls, as she would find out much later, and the helicopter had been tasked with trying to find him.

But directly ahead she went, right into one of the propellers.

Since she was a fairy, and fairies are immortal, the helicopter didn't do much damage. It did, however, manage to fling Tink far into the distance, over the top of the falls and Grand Island and Buffalo and all the way to the woods of middle-of-nowhere New York, until she crashed through a layer of trees and down, down, down to the ferns that caught her in their fronds.

For a while, she lay there in the dark, listening to animals scurry over branches and watching the bugs flitter across the face of the moon. After some time she heard a voice calling out, but instead of her name, the voice was insistently repeating "Michael? Michael, come out, come out, wherever you are. Michael? This isn't funny, Michael."

"Hello?" Tink said during a pause between Michaels.

"Hello?" the voice said back.

A light emerged in the trees and drew closer. There were two heads, one belonging to a boy of about fifteen and one to a girl a few years older than that. The girl had the flashlight, which she shone into Tink's eyes until Tink asked whether she could turn the damn thing off or at least stop blinding Tink with it.

"Language," the girl scolded.

If Tink was feeling up to it, she would have given the girl a certain finger, but she could only weakly blink.

"Why do you look so strange?" the boy asked Tink.

For a moment she wondered about her wings, but luckily they were only visible to other fairies or those under the influence of their dust. He must have been referring to her outfit, she realized, a green dress the color of a new leaf and little yellow slippers with flowers blooming on the toes. Tink hated her "costume," as she called it when complaining to Peter, but she never knew when her Godmother—the fairy in charge of making sure her girls were properly dressed and always behaving in a manner befitting such a magical species—might drop in.

"Why do *you* look so strange?" Tink asked back. And he did, in his old man's button-up shirt and pressed trousers.

The girl gave the boy the flashlight and instructed him to keep the beam on Tink. The girl's face was suddenly illuminated, and in that moment, the entire forest went quiet. It was like Tink had been standing next to a speaker at a concert and then stepped outside, or like she had been submerged in the ocean, or like . . . nothing she had ever felt before. The soft brown hair trimmed neatly at the girl's shoulders, the delicate tilt of her nose, the sweater buttoned all the way up to her throat: three tiny paintings that separately might not account for much but that together cause an onlooker to stop and wonder at their microcosmic world.

Then the girl bent down out of the light, so that her face was a few inches from the fairy, and examined her by first moving one arm, then the other. One leg, then the other. One eye, tested with two fingers, then the other.

"No permanent damage," the girl declared, and slid her forearm under Tink in order to hoist her up.

Normally, Tink would have made a joke about permanent damage not being permanent—she liked to point out when people said stupid things—but she found that she couldn't say much beyond yes, and thank you, and Michael who? She had even forgotten about Peter.

"Michael is our brother," the girl said.

"And I'm John Darling," the boy said proudly.

"Who are you calling darling?" Tink scowled, though he probably couldn't see her.

"It's our last name," the girl said. Her laugh was like a little bell ringing at the opening of a door. "He's John Darling, and I'm Wendy Darling, and Michael, wherever he's gotten off to, is Michael Darling."

"Oh. Right." Tink refrained from saying how unfortunate it was to have such a confusing last name. "I'm Tinker Bell. Two words, one first name, before you ask."

Wendy laughed again, as if Tink had made a joke, and then she and John helped Tink walk back through the woods toward a light in the distance. On the way they passed several oddities, including a cottage their father had built as a playhouse before he got sick, and the cemetery where their mother was buried. Tink took to the cottage right away, with its quaint thatched roof and round door—probably because it reminded her of her own home back in Neverland—but she was too sore to explore it further. Plus, it had been left in disrepair since their father's illness, said Wendy, pointing out the hole where mice had chewed through the dry reeds.

The main house was much larger, but equally shabby. The light illuminating the porch was missing its glass sconce, the rocking chair's wicker had fallen through its frame, one of the windows was taped closed with a layer of plastic, and weeds had taken up residence in every flowerbed.

"What a lovely home," Tink said.

"It isn't, really," Wendy said, "but you're kind to say so."

"We do our best," John added.

Wendy didn't want to risk waking her father, so she and John set Tink down on the porch step next to a pile of black-and-white fur that turned out to be a dog. Nana was old, John said, or else she would have been out looking for Michael along with the rest of them.

"I should get back," Wendy said, her eyes back on the woods. "Michael loves to play hide and seek, but he won't come out no matter how long we look. Do you know, one time back in London he hid in a trash bin behind a bakery for eight whole hours? The collector found him there the next morning, asleep on the stale rolls."

"He sounds like he's a Lost Boy," Tink said.

" . . . He is lost," John said, looking down at Tink through his black-framed glasses. "That's what we've been telling you."

Before Tink could explain—which, on further reflection, she probably wouldn't have anyway for risk of sounding even crazier than they already thought her—two dark figures came out of the woods and became a little boy of about five and a familiar older boy in a red tunic decorated in leaves.

"Peter!" Tink exclaimed, remembering him all at once.

"Tink!" Peter rushed to her side. "How funny, that you're in the exact last place I expected to find you. Are you hurt, Tink? Can you—"

He was probably going to say fly, but he remembered their company and closed his lips tight.

"I'll be alright," Tink said bravely. She was fine, with the exception of a headache and a sore arm, but it was nice having people worry over her.

She soon realized, however, that Peter was no longer worrying about her or even looking at her. Another girl, almost a woman, had caught his eye.

"Peter Pan," Peter said. He took off his cap and bowed, as though he were a gentleman asking a lady to dance.

"Wendy Darling." Wendy curtsied.

"What is this, the Victorian era?" Tink said loudly, but either no one heard her or they'd chosen to ignore her.

She had a bad feeling about this meeting, very bad, and it was not improved by little Michael, who sat down next to her on the step with a thump and, touching his chubby hand to her cheek, asked in an innocent voice whether this was the kind of fairy who granted wishes or the kind who made Christmas presents in the North Pole.

"You mean elves," John corrected, "and you're old enough to know that she's just a girl in a Halloween costume."

"But Halloween was last week," Michael insisted. Everyone ignored him, and Tink breathed a sigh of relief.

When Wendy asked where Peter and Tink were from, Peter said just down the road and Tink said Canada. They looked at each other and then said in unison, *Just down the road, in Canada, eh?* Tink felt a little bit better—after all, no goody-goody could replace her as Peter's partner in crime—and Peter even winked at her when no one else was looking.

"Would you like to come in for some tea before you go back?" Wendy asked.

"I don't think we shou—" Tink started to say, but Peter interrupted her with an enthusiastic *Absolutely!* even though he always said tea was for boring grown-ups.

A bad feeling . . . very bad.

The house was old and full of strange trinkets, like an oil lamp and a typewriter and a wood burning stove. "Papa used to have an affinity for antiques," Wendy said, as though her father were already dead. The inside of the house was as shoddy as the outside, but the kitchen, where Wendy led them, was kept clean by Wendy's busy hands. No sooner had she put a kettle on the stove then she was washing five mugs, putting cookies on a plate, sweeping up the crumbs with the back of her porcelain hand, and wiping Michael's mouth with a linen tea towel.

"Delicious," Peter said, though Tink hadn't seen him take a single sip from the blue mug steaming in front of him. Later, he would dump the tea down the sink when only Tink was looking. Tink, on the other hand, loved the taste of chamomile, especially after such an exhausting night. Her eyes blinked, blinked, closed, and she had to pinch herself to get them open again.

"Look," Michael said, and he pointed to Tink. "The fairy girl is falling asleep."

"It's been a long day," Peter said, as though to excuse her for some rudeness, and Tink thought, *Who do you think you're fooling, Peter Pan?* This was a boy who fell asleep with his head on the table and a glass of nectar in his hand almost nightly. "Maybe we could stay here for the night?"

Instantly, Tink was wide awake. Stay here? In the real world? Beyond the strangeness of staying in a creepy old house like this one, there was the obvious problem of needing to return Peter to Neverland to keep him immortal.

"But Peter—" Tink began.

"Of course you can stay!" Wendy declared, and Michael clapped his chubby hands together in glee. "I'll make up the guest bedrooms at once. John, Michael, come help with the corners of the bedsheets. No, no," she said when Tink started to rise, "not you two. You're our guests."

As soon as the Darlings were out of earshot, Tink launched into her tirade. "Peter Pan, you naughty boy, you know very well that we can't stay in the real world for even a single night without—"

"Quick," Peter interrupted, "before she gets back, I have to tell you something very important." He tipped his tea down the sink, put the mug back in its place on the table, and then leaned in very close so that Tink could smell the mist of the falls in his clothes. "I'm in love."

When Tink looks back on that moment, she can recall every detail. The timid whistling of the just-boiling teapot. The rough surface of the wooden table grooved by so many family dinners. The sound of footsteps above their heads as the Darlings prepared their beds. When Tink looks back on that moment she freezes it there, like pausing a movie—but in the real world life goes on.

Tink knows that better than anyone.

"Oh good, the water is ready," Wendy said as she drifted back into the kitchen with John and Michael at her heels. "More tea, anyone?"

Peter lifted his mug enthusiastically.

CHAPTER FOUR

"Founding of the Home Under the Ground"

Excerpt from *Neverland: A History*

AFTER THE FAIRIES CREATED A LIVABLE geography and populated it with the oppressed groups mentioned in previous chapters (see "Mermaids" and "Native People of Kandallan"), they still had room in the forest quadrant of Neverland for more creatures. Many petitioned for land, but it just so happened that the Queen's daughter, Princess Fern, had recently been on a mission trip to the real world and attached herself to the cause of the orphans of that realm. "Why not give the land to them?" she asked, and since her mother's hundred-year reign was almost up, the Queen decided to indulge Princess Fern's request.

There were, of course, stipulations.

Seeing as how anyone in the magical realm was immortal—as long as they didn't get stabbed, or eaten by a crocodile, or otherwise maimed or mortally wounded—they could not allow members of both sexes to dwell in Neverland. Just as the mermaids had only girls, the Home Under the Ground would have only boys. The Kandallanians were still a concern, of course, but seeing as they only reproduced every two hundred years, the fairies gave them a population quota and land on Mars to which they might send their additional members. (Note: The ritual for selecting which Kandallanian babies remain in Neverland is a fascinating one, but unfortunately, outside of the scope of this history—for more resources, read *The True Story of Kandallan.*)

Besides the stipulation about the gender of its inhabitants, the Home Under the Ground had other rules. They would have a leader, much like the Fairy Queen, who would be responsible for the general goings-on of the group; that leader would be assigned a member of the fairy guard to advise him on proper behavior, as well as take him on occasional journeys to the real world to rescue more orphans up to but never to exceed one hundred. After that, members who wanted to return to the real world could be substituted for a new child, provided the fairy guard wiped the older member's memory.

The fairy guard was, under no circumstances, to allow her charge to remain in the real world longer than a single night.

The fairy guard was, under no circumstances, to allow her charge to speak to or otherwise interact with anyone above the age of sixteen, which was the age when Lost Boys reached maturity.

The fairy guard was, under no circumstances, to fall in love with the leader of the group that would come to be called the Lost Boys.

Not that the last rule was every explicitly stated, of course.

But it should have been understood.

CHAPTER FIVE

Now

THE DARLING HOUSE, NOW CALLED THE Haunted Mansion, sits in the forest bed like an old woman resting in a bundle of blankets. Technically the house belongs to John and Michael, but they haven't been back in almost forty years. Still, the house is owned, and therefore it cannot be condemned.

Most days Tink hurries past the gate askew on its hinges, but today she rests her bucket next to the unmarked mailbox and follows the path of tall grass to the porch. One of the stairs has fallen in, leaving a gap like Michael used to have between his two front teeth. The last time Tink saw him, Michael had grown into a broad-shouldered athlete in a sleeveless T-shirt, and he was raking the leaves from around the cherry tree where they buried Nana. It was autumn, which meant the leaves were still falling, and they rained down around him as he raked and raked at the same spot until the grass came up too. John was on the porch reading a textbook of some kind, and he didn't look up when Michael let out a stream of curses that even Tink couldn't repeat. Poor Michael, motherless a second time, about to enter the world of college without anyone but awkward John to offer him a word of advice.

Tink had wanted to say hello, but instead she pulled her sweatshirt up over her head and hurried on her way. The boys could not be allowed to recognize her—after all, while they had grown into men, she had stayed exactly the same. Peter needed Neverland to keep his face fresh, but a fairy was a fairy no matter where she rested her wings.

The next year, they both left, and the following summer neither of them came back.

Now, the leaves hide like river sediment under a layer of melting snow. Tink knocks on the door and then turns the doorknob, unlocked since the first time she broke in through a basement window. The foyer is silent; the clocks have long since stopped their ticking. The carpets are muddy and worn. Without Wendy, everything in the house has fallen into disarray—Tink included.

Tink goes upstairs to the line of bedroom doors and names them: Wendy's father, Wendy, John, Michael, Peter, Tink. She goes into the room that was hers, if only for a brief time, but there is little to distinguish the drab curtains and four poster bed as anything but a guest bedroom. Tink skips Peter's room and checks in on Michael's football posters, John's shelves of books, and Wendy's flowery bedspread. Wendy loved the washed-out roses and matched everything in the room to their delicate petals, from her cream desk to her pink curtains. When she lay in the center of the queen bed, stomach against the fabric and legs crossed above her, she had looked more fairylike than Tink.

Following her path—and stalling for time—Tink enters the master suite of Mr. Darling. Tink had not seen him much, except as a pale hand on a curtain the times he watched his children playing in the yard or a shadow tucked into royal blue sheets. Mr. Darling died soon after Wendy's funeral, but by then Tink had moved into the cottage on the edge of the property, and besides, the arrangements were for a closed casket.

Despite his illness, Mr. Darling had loved to read the paper, and Wendy or John had brought him the news with his breakfast daily. Up to date on current events, yet unaware that a fairy and a wild boy had taken up residence in his house. Tink fingers through the tall stack of yellowed papers on the nightstand, finding completed crosswords and articles with key phrases underlined with two bold strokes, and then returns them to their teetering tower. Then she turns the closet light on and inspects the dusty wool blazers with elbow patches, which he must have worn during his teaching days. Such an intelligent man must have realized there were unfamiliar voices calling out Marco and Polo around his house; such an intelligent man must have been curious at the thunderous sound of five sets of feet racing downstairs for first choice of Danish butter cookie shape.

Stop stalling, Tink thinks. With a sigh, she turns off the light and closes Mr. Darling's door behind her.

At Peter's door, Tink presses her small hand against the green paint and pauses there, imagining Peter doing the same on the other side. Death was just a waterfall, and if she squinted hard enough, Peter's shadow would become visible from the other side. Yet when she opens the door, there is no one.

Peter's room looks like Neverland from a great height. *Home,* Tink used to think every time she spotted the lagoon, and now she sees the same body of water painted on the far wall. To the right is Neverwood, where below ground the Lost Boys would be waiting in The Home Under the Ground. To the left is Marooners' Rock. Peter did not have a talent for art, and Tink wonders if Wendy helped him—and if she did help him, how could she imagine, with such accuracy, the tiny Jolly Roger or the wings of the Never bird? And if she had imagined them, what had she thought of Peter's stories, so specific, so far from the reality of her dreary life? Had they charmed her? Had they made her uneasy?

Tink will never know the answers to these questions. She had been surprised to find the mural after John and Michael left the house and she made her first pilgrimage to her original earthly home. No, surprised is not the right word—distraught is more like it. She had been distraught that Peter had missed Neverland so much, when for all Tink had known, he had abandoned their home without so much as a backward glance. Why hadn't he talked to her about it? Why hadn't he confided in her?

Oh, please. You know exactly why.

This voice was in her head, and yet it also came from the dark place on the wall where her shadow lingered over the green canopy of the Never trees. Fairies weren't supposed to have shadows—too easy to catch a creature with a shadow—and yet there she was, a black cut-out of Tink as she was supposed to look: green leaf dress, toned legs, impressive wings. Even the sight of those expansive appendages made Tink shudder. She doesn't fly anymore; she doesn't have wings anymore. Speaking of which . . .

Tink slides out of her coat and dirty black t-shirt. In the mirror over Peter's desk—which she is confident he never used—Tink eyes the nubs of bone and yellow gossamer emerging like a tentative shoot from a seed. So determined, yet Tink is more determined still. From the pocket of her coat she removes a glass vial full of acid, fills the dropper, and, using the mirror to guide her, lets a few droplets fall on her newly forming wings.

There is no one left in the mansion to hear her screams.

CHAPTER SIX

Then

"PETER PAN," TINK HISSED UNDER THE covers of her bed, where she and Peter had taken refuge to talk about their plan, "you know very well that you can't stay in the real world for even one night."

"I know, I know," Peter said, and yet Tink had the feeling there was a *but* coming. "But what harm can one night really do?"

"What harm?" Tink's voice went up an octave. "You are literally aging every minute we spend here. Already, you are four hours older. And in four more hours, you'll be eight hours older. And four more hours after that—"

"Alright, alright, no need to show off," said Peter, who didn't know math or geography or any subjects but flying and managing the Lost Boys. "But Tink, I'm—"

"In love. I know. You've literally already told me a hundred times." Tink tried—and failed—to hide her skepticism. At least Peter couldn't see her rolling eyes. The air under the covers was getting hot and moist from too much breath, and Tink wasn't sure whether that or Peter's proclaimed love was making her feel sick. "But Peter, you've only known this girl for what, two seconds? You were charmed by her pretty hair, her delicate hands, her whispery voice—"

"I didn't mention any of those things, Tink. I was actually captivated by her beautiful brown eyes."

Tink was glad Peter was not the kind of boy who thought too hard.

"But think of the Lost Boys, Peter," she pressed on. "Think of how worried they'll be when they don't see that familiar green ghost and his attractive fairy sidekick flying overhead. Think of how abandoned they'll feel when they realize we're not coming back."

Peter didn't say anything for a minute. Tink was sweating so much her "costume" was drenched. The shimmery fringe bit into her sore arms. She wanted to change into the spare nightgown Wendy had left on the corner of the bed, but convincing Peter was taking longer than she'd hoped.

"You're right," he finally said. Tink couldn't see Peter's face, but he sounded sincere.

"I am?"

"Absolutely. You always know the right thing to do, Tink. You can go back to Neverland and tell the Lost Boys where I am, and then you can come back and get me."

"That isn't what I—"

"You're the best, Tink."

Peter touched her sweaty arm, and Tink forgot whatever argument she might have made. Then he threw the covers back like Houdini whipping off a tablecloth, blasting them both with cool air. Before Tink could come up with a reason for him not to stay, Peter had leapt off the bed and skipped through the door, down the hall, and into his own bedroom. The door closed with an enthusiastic smack.

Tink had no choice but to delicately slide off the bed—she was still injured, after all—and place herself in a convenient take-off location. At least the windows were large casement windows that opened by a crank, not those unfortunate double-hung windows where she had to slide one up and dangle precariously out the opening and then throw herself out like a fish returned to water. Still, the air was cold on her wet skin, and the wind had picked up, and there was no light for miles to guide her way. Tink put a foot up on the sill, noting her wet and muddy slipper, and leaned her weight on the heel. *Taking off in five, four, three, two—*

Half-launched, Tink froze. Her body, balanced on the sill, swayed precariously. What was she thinking? If she returned to Neverland and told the Lost Boys about Peter, then he would feel no need to return. But if she left the task to him, the guilt for his boys would eventually wear him down. All Tink needed to do was get him back to Neverland—the island would do the rest.

This was not, after all, the first time Peter had been enamored with the real world. There was that time with his birth mother when he vowed to return and stay with her, until he found out she had a new baby to love. He had once spent two days on Coney Island, enjoying the rides both day and night. Peter was like a myna bird entertained by whatever bell or mirror appeared in front of him. Soon enough, a new toy would draw his fancy, and he would return to Neverland without a second thought.

Or at least that's what Tink told herself as she climbed up onto the bed and rested her weary limbs, laying on top of the comforter to allow her wings full stretch.

The next morning, she felt revived. Her worries had subsided; her aches had followed suit. The Darling house seemed lighter, less dusty, more pleasantly filled with children playing at house in the kitchen. Tink, forgetting that she was still in Wendy's nightgown, followed the smell of toast and marmalade downstairs, where chaos met her happy face.

"Duck, Tink!" Peter instructed. Without a moment's hesitation, Tink sunk to her knees. A burnt crust flew past her head, hit the wall, and fell into the trash can accompanied by a spray of black crumbs.

"Sorry!" said John, not sounding at all sorry.

"I want to do it too," Michael insisted, but his crust, even without the obstacle of Tink, only made it a few feet in the right direction. Nana, who had been asleep on the rug, lifted her head to sniff at the bread and then ate it.

"Watch a pro," Peter bragged. He bent off a large slice of his toast, pulled his arm back like a pitcher, and let the piece fly. It soared beautifully, a spaceship headed for an unknown destination, and went right out the open window. "But . . . " Peter said, looking distraught, "back home I always—"

"—Have a full breakfast in you first," Tink interrupted, before he could mention the name of Neverland or the magic it contained. "Eat up, Peter Pan, and then you'll surely make the shot."

"Tink is right," Wendy said. She brought a pan of scrambled eggs to the table, and the boys dug their forks in without waiting for a serving spoon. "Food first, then play."

"Alright, Wendy," Peter Pan said, properly chastised.

Tink might have commented on the fact that it was she, not Wendy, who had made the pronouncement, but then Wendy winked at her in a way that said, *At least we know better.* She made the two girls their own eggs, and Tink forgot all about her troubles as she sat quietly with Wendy and listened to the boys planning out their day.

"First we have to sweep the sidewalk," John instructed, "and then pack the lunches. Michael, maybe you can feed the dog? Peter, you can make the beds—"

"Or," said Peter, holding his fork up like he was a judge raising his gavel to pound for order, "instead of all of that boring stuff, we could make leaf piles in the front yard and jump into them. Then, we could fix up that old treehouse in the backyard, the one—"

"Silly Peter," said Wendy. "It's a school day!"

"School?"

"Exactly. And speaking of which, won't they be missing you at your own school?"

"Uh . . . " Peter looked at Tink.

"We are on fall break," Tink explained. "It's . . . a . . . Canadian thing."

"I must admit, I don't know much about Canada," Wendy said. "Father never took us there after we moved back to the United States, and then . . . he . . . you understand. When does your break end?"

"January," Peter said, before Tink could say November. "January fifteenth."

"Oh good," Wendy said. She smiled shyly at Peter. "Maybe you can stay with us until then? Consider it a study abroad program."

"Oh yes, of cou—"

"We'll have to ask our parents," Tink said, again saving Peter from incriminating them.

"Right," Peter agreed. "Our parents. But they'll definitely say yes."

And so, Tink and Peter became wards of the Darling house—at least until Tink could think of a way to get them back to Neverland. The day darkened once more. After the other children left, Tink told Peter that she needed to go on a long walk to clear her head, and then she set out on a journey to explore the Darling's large backyard.

CHAPTER SEVEN

"Tinker Bell"

Excerpt from in *Neverland: A History*

We are lucky enough to have, in our possession, Tinker Bell's original application for the royal guard. This questionnaire is administered to all potential members, and though the questions occasionally change, they are carefully crafted by a committee of five senior officers of the fairy guard—me being one of them—in order to perfectly place each dedicated fairy in the right position for them.

Name:
Tinker Bell

Address:
If you need me, you can find me at my stall.

Date of Blossoming:
28 April 1771

In a hundred words, please describe, in detail, your reasons for applying to the fairy guard:
You asked me to.

Please list your preferred posts, as selected from the extensive organization chart on page 3 of this application.

Any that don't involve sweeping pollen or collecting sap. Oh, and no giant squirrels. I hate giant squirrels.

Please list what you see as your greatest strengths:

What is this, a therapy session? I don't know—I guess I'd say tinkering, mending, and securing payments from customers. But unless the Queen needs her pots fixed, I don't see how those will be relevant.

Please list what you see as your greatest weaknesses:

If I don't get the job, you can tell me.

CHAPTER EIGHT

Now

TINK SLIDES THE VIAL INTO HER coat pocket and gets dressed. The sun has begun to melt the snow on the roof, which is now dripping steadily onto the gablet of the window and then the roof of the porch below. Tink should go—she has a lot of drinking to do before sunset—but she lingers at the mural on her way out. Her pointer finger finds the place where the Home Under the Ground would be, and she strokes the raised paint of the tree leaves. How long it must have taken Peter to dutifully mark every one, until the branches were sufficiently covered and the Home was hidden from view. But he knew it was there, and Tink knows it's there, and so she rubs at the place where her heart wants to go.

Wait.

Is that the paint chipping? Or maybe . . .

Part of the wall—the paper covering one side of the gypsum—comes away in her hand, leaving some bare drywall with scratches on its pale face. Ink markings, she realizes, and though she never saw Peter write a letter, she somehow knows the lines belong to him.

Here lies Home, which no home can replace.

Tink drops the paper onto the wood floor, where the paint and gypsum break into crumbs. She is surprised; she is angry. *Who do you think you are, Peter Pan?* she rants. *You can't have it all. You can't call Neverland your home, yet abandon it so—*

She starts to cry, but then brushes her face with her dirty sleeve and forces herself to stop. Peter made his choice. Peter chose Wendy. These are the facts; the message, maybe meant for Tink to find one day, is the dream. So many years have passed, and yet one small reminder of Peter still sends her into a depression that lasts for days. *Why even go on living?* she thinks in those times, and yet she knows she cannot die, even if she wanted to. She is cursed to this lonely life, to this home which will never be Home.

"Hello?"

Tink freezes. She often talks to herself, but this voice is not hers—real or imagined. There is someone else in the Darling house. There is little in Peter's room to use as a weapon, so Tink removes the shade from the bedside lamp and carries it down the hallway by the base. A careful knock of the head, a swing to a kneecap, a—

"Hello?"

Tink leans over the banister and looks down. There is a girl there about Tink's age. She wears a black pea coat, some kind of black tights, and black leather boots with two-inch heels. No one wears boots like that here—too impractical. One slip out the door and you're facing a slow death by freezing. Her hair is red and straight. Her ears shine with sparkly studs.

Focus, Tink thinks. The girl is probably twice Tink's size, and Tink looks skeptically at her lamp. Perhaps if she dropped the lamp from the second floor, the heavy metal might—

"God, you scared me." The girl is looking up at Tink, who is apparently less well hidden than she thought. "I was afraid you were some pack of teenage boys messing up the place, or maybe a murderer, or . . . Who are you, anyway?"

"Uh . . . " Tink puts the lamp down out of sight and slides it over further with her foot. "I'm Tink."

"Tink?"

"That's right."

"Well, *Tink*," the girl says, as though she doesn't believe that Tink's name is really Tink, "I'm Hope. It's been a pleasure meeting you, but I'm tired, so if you'd be so kind, I'd like the house to myself."

Hope removes her coat and hangs it on the hook by the door, as though she's just come home from a long day. Then she unzips her boots, revealing bright pink socks.

"Excuse me," Tink says, "but before you make yourself at home, *Hope*, I have a few questions for—"

"No, you don't." Hope's voice is less kind now.

"Yes, I do," Tink insists. She is perfectly capable of serving that tone right back.

Suddenly, Hope rushes up the stairs. Her journey brings her height into such greater clarity, Tink thinks, *This girl's taller than Captain Hook.*

"No," Hope says, reaching the landing and now towering over the fairy. Up close, she smells like some kind of apple spray. "You don't. This is my house, and that makes you my guest. Consider this your warning, baby girl, leave now, or I'll throw you out myself."

Tink should leave, but she's never been good at following orders. Peter knew this well—anytime he needed Tink to do anything, he had the smallest Lost Boys ask her, so that their pleading little eyes made saying no less satisfying.

"Consider this your warning, big girl," Tink says, and she plows forward though even she knows she's going to lose. "This house belongs to the Darlings, so unless you bought it with money from your piggy bank, I'd ask you to please vacate the premises before I have to . . . " Saying *throw you out* to someone she can't lift seems ridiculous, even by Tink's standards, so she ends lamely with, " . . . chase you out."

Tink's face is mere inches from Hope's at this point. The two girls stare each other down, neither of them blinking for over a minute. Hope's breath betrays the apple cider she must have had on her trip. Her eyes are dark brown, like two holes in the dirt. Tink wonders if she can really take Hope down, and decides that she probably can't.

Then Hope starts laughing.

"God, you're strange," she says, and loses their staring contest when she looks away. "You look like a little doll, but then surprise, you can put up a fight. If you must know, Tink, I *am* a Darling. Hope Darling, or at least that would have been my name if my father hadn't been adopted. Wendy Darling was my grandmother—it says so right in my father's adoption file."

Tink suddenly feels faint. *Hope Darling. Father's file.* Her empty stomach and alcohol-induced headache are back, but worse. She holds onto Hope for support, and the girl leans Tink against the wall and then down to the floor to catch her breath.

"You can't be . . . " Tink whispers.

But she knows, with sudden clarity, that Hope can.

CHAPTER NINE

Then

It was after the Darlings left for school and Tink went on her walk that she found, again, the cottage with the balding straw roof. Tink didn't know why the little house appealed to her so much, or why, when she wanted so badly to break up Peter and Wendy, she even considered leaving them alone together in the big house. Maybe she had already accepted that there was little she could do while Wendy and Peter had their fun; maybe she was just a solitary creature, used to living in her own little apartment in Neverland. Either way, she decided to fix up the place, just in case she ever needed her own thinking spot.

The door was open, so Tink went inside. The condition she found there was worse than the outside, since the loosely fitted door had let in all kinds of leaves and bugs and wet forest scents. The cottage was made up of one central room, in which there was a bare daybed with a mattress that sagged in the middle, a wobbly wooden table, and three chairs; a bathroom with only a toilet and sink so small that even Tink had to hold her arms near her sides to fit; and a kitchen made up of a mini fridge, double burner stove and two cabinets full of antique plates and glass cups Mr. Darling had probably bought for a few dollars at a thrift store. Someone could survive here—but they wouldn't want to.

Unless that someone was Tink.

Though the fairy loved to fly anywhere she pleased, she preferred to live in smaller quarters. She was like a bird on her nest, or an owl in her hole, or a bear in her cave. A small space is safe; a small space can be protected. And fairies were somewhere on the spectrum between humans and animals, their natural instincts not completely quieted by the greediness of mankind.

Yes, she thought as she sat on the sagging bed, *I could be very comfortable here.*

After she snuck back into the main house for supplies—Peter, playing darts with the boys, was too busy to notice—Tink returned to the cottage with a broom and dustbin to do a clean sweep of the floor. She wiped the windows until she could see in all directions—she wanted to be prepared for any visitors, invited or not—and fixed the door in the frame. One steak knife she found in the drawer would serve as a weapon. In time, she could perhaps fashion some arrows and a little bow.

"Tink?" a voice called, and Tink immediately ran from the cottage in the opposite direction. By the time Peter stumbled onto her location, she had climbed halfway up a tree. "What are you doing up there?" Peter asked, and Tink opened her hand, showing him a few sour apples.

Peter bent his knees and kicked off, hopping a little and then landing hard.

"You're not going to fly very far without fairy dust," Tink teased.

"Oh come on, Tink," he whined, and Tink wiped a wing with her right pointer finger and rubbed the dust so that it fell like snow on Peter's head. Up he came, alighting on the same branch, and soon enough they had both eaten their fill of the fruit most humans found to be too sour raw.

"These apples make me think of Never fruit," Tink said. "Remember how the Lost Boys used to see who could throw them the farthest?"

"Do I remember? Of course I remember." Peter thrust out his chest. "It was me!"

"I'd forgotten," said Tink, even though of course she hadn't. "I wonder what the boys are doing right now."

"Me too." Peter looked off into the distance. Tink wondered if he could almost hear the call of the boys up in the trees, the way she could. Any minute, one of them might attack with an onslaught of overripe berries. "What did they say when you told them?"

"Uh . . . " Tink turned an apple around and around in her hand. "I didn't."

"Tink!"

"If you want to stay here and grow into a man," Tink said, "then you'd better start acting like one and tell them yourself."

This seemed to stump Peter. Likely he hadn't thought through what all of this growing up would mean—that one day he would look in the mirror and see someone old enough to be a father. That one day, he would be too old to reenter Neverland, even if he wanted to.

"I love her," Peter said. Then he dropped the rest of his apples on the ground and floated down after them.

"More than you love your boys?" Tink yelled, but Peter had already begun to walk away and pretended not to hear her.

* * *

When the Darlings returned from school, John and Michael immediately pounced on Peter, begging him to wrestle. "Homework first," Wendy chastised.

"Oh come on, Wendy," whined Michael, "Can't we play for just a little while?"

"Yeah, Wendy, don't they get a break?" Peter asked.

"Homework first," Wendy repeated.

The three students went to the dining room, where John and Michael spread out their binders, books, and pencils on the table and Wendy sat in the bay window with a book in her lap. Tink was curious, so she hovered over their shoulders, trying to make out what schools taught these days.

"What's that chapter about?" she asked Michael. The pictures in his book were of some strange-looking dead people in capsules.

"Mummies," said Michael. He pointed to a word in large red print at the top of the page. "Can't you read, Tink?"

Wendy and John looked up from their books.

"Of course I can," Tink said. She laughed a little too loudly. "I just wanted to see if you could."

In reality, none of Neverland's inhabitants knew how to read or write. Of course some of the Lost Boys had come to the island with a few years of learning in them, but what scholastic abilities they had were lost over the years. Neverland had a way of making you forget everything you'd ever known, and though Tink was immune to its charms, she'd never learned in the first place.

"Tink, why don't you come sit with me?" Wendy asked.

Wendy moved her feet a little to make room for Tink, who climbed onto the seat and perched there like a bird on a branch. She began to read from the pages in front of her, and Tink closed her eyes in order to visualize what she heard.

Over hill, over dale,
Through bush, through brier,
Over park, over pale,
Through flood, through fire,
I do wander everywhere,
Swifter than the moon's sphere;
And I serve the fairy queen,
To dew her orbs upon the green.
The cowslips tall her pensioners be:
In their gold coats spots you see;
Those be rubies, fairy favours,
In those freckles live their savours:
I must go seek some dewdrops here
And hang a pearl in every cowslip's ear.
Farewell, thou lob of spirits; I'll be gone:
Our queen and all our elves come here anon.

Tink couldn't help bursting into laughter. "What nonsense is this?" she asked. "Pearls and rubies? Why would fairies wear such heavy objects when they're supposed to be 'swifter than the moon's sphere,' whatever that means?

And by the way, who are these elves you speak of? No one but fairies enters or leaves the kingdom, so how would they go anywhere with the Queen, whose duty it is to keep watch over that realm?"

"It's Shakespeare," said Wendy. She gave Tink a strange look. "Fairies aren't real, Tink."

"Of course they're not," said Tink, "but that doesn't mean this Shakespeare character couldn't write a more believable story."

Wendy continued to read out loud, and several times Tink had to bite the inside of her lips to keep from speaking out about some error or another. In the end she gave up listening and focused on just the sound of Wendy's voice, soft but clear, and the way that the leaves drifted from the trees and danced across the grass at the same tempo. She thought of the Lost Boys, and how she used to tell them stories every night before bed and timed them to the exact moment the coals of the fire went dark. *How they must miss her,* she thought, and then a worse thought overwhelmed her: Would Neverland erase their memory of Tink, too?

"Tink?" Wendy asked. She put her hand on Tink's bare knee, and the fairy shivered. "Are you alright?"

"Fine," she said. "Just keep reading."

Wendy went on, and Tink's mind drifted up, up, up through the setting sun and the clouds hanging like ghosts, and then down again, to the kingdom where fairies live, a castle whittled from a willow-like tree whose locks of leaves protect the fairies from discovery and hide their light. A long time ago Tink lived there too, back when she spent her days mending pots and returning them to the richer fairy folk who had their servants slip a warm coin into her palm. A worker fairy, a common fairy, one puzzle piece that made up the greater kingdom. And there she would have stayed, tinkering at kettles, if one of the Godmothers had not come to Tink to mend her own pot and neglected to pay her.

Consider it your duty to the crown, the Godmother had told Tink, reaching for her now perfectly round kettle.

Tink's hand snapped out to the Godmother's wrist and held it. *You're not the Queen,* she said. *The Queen insists on honesty and fair compensation for all fairies. You're nothing but a fat, lazy excuse for a royal servant. You should be ashamed to sully the Queen's good name in this way, you vile, villainous lump of—*

The Godmother raised her hand to strike the insolent fairy, but another Godmother in her telltale blue dress stopped her with a sharp whistle. *You forget your place, Godmother Jane,* the second Godmother said, and Godmother Jane huffed and then hurried away, minus her kettle.

I'm sorry for my rudeness, Tink said, her eyes lowered to her tools so as not to make eye contact with such a high-ranking official. *It's just that she wasn't going to pay me, and then she used the Queen's name as explanation, and I couldn't just stand there and—*

Quiet, the second Godmother said, forcefully but not unkindly. Tink looked up and noticed that the Godmother seemed to be examining her. *You're quite rambunctious for a common light. But now that I think of it, I happen to have need of just such a fairy. How would you like to leave these pots behind and come work for me?*

How would she like it? Tink dropped her hammer right then, and she never picked it up again. The Godmother, who said her name was Godmother Anne, gave Tink the uniform of the royal guard and sent her to Neverland to look after a boy named Peter who had given the other fairies quite a bit of trouble. Tink still remembers her first day on the job, when upon her arrival the Lost Boys assailed her with overripe tomatoes and filled her entire house with water by plugging the windows and door with moss and then threading a hose down the chimney. Maybe most fairies would have flown right back to the castle and asked to be reassigned, but Tink was not "most fairies." She was not, as Godmother Anne had recognized, a "common light." She was the kind of fairy who exacted her revenge swiftly, so that when the Lost Boys went home to celebrate, they found their own lair under attack from a thousand flying toads Tink had enchanted with her fairy dust.

From that day on, they'd been a family.

And no matter what it takes or who I have to take down in the process, Tink thought as Wendy closed her book and smiled at her window companion, *I'm going to make sure we stay that way.*

CHAPTER TEN

"Flora and Fauna"

Excerpt from *Neverland: A History*

ANY CELESTIAL BODY REQUIRES A CAREFUL balancing of flora and fauna in order to help the planet thrive; in the case of the creation of Neverland, this equation was even more important since, as I mentioned in previous chapters, all creatures were immortal unless eaten or mortally maimed. The Queen—or rather her team of advisors, who had more time to dedicate to the Neverland exercise—partnered with thirty-five wildlife biologists and zoologists from the more intellectually advanced planet of Tag to monitor every aspect of Neverland. There was everyone from an expert in mermaid diets to a PhD in human customs, a lifelong birder to an intern who collected reptile feces and analyzed the contents in one of Tag's state-of-the-art labs.

What we discovered—or what the members of the Tag team discovered and then relayed to the fairies in simpler language—was that Neverland needed little help in maintaining its ecosystem. Since the flora and fauna were modelled after those of Earth, they took their rightful place in the food chain in the same fashion: the Never birds, a breed of hawks with purple feathers, ate the mice; the mice ate the seeds from the purple fruit of the Never trees. So on and so on, predator to prey.

After a while, the team from Tag went home, and we left Neverland to its fate.

Then, reports from the guard in what would become Tinker Bell's position came in: the toads, who should have been primary food for the slithery snakes who sunned themselves all day on Marooners' Rock, were moving inland and eating the worms who lived on the sour Never fruit instead of the insects near the water. Thus, they had lost their flavor, and the slithery snakes were eating more of the mice than normal. This new habit affected the birds, who were mostly still alive but emaciated and rarely able to fly more than a hundred feet.

In the world of wildlife biology, that summer—which would later be referred to as Toad Summer—was a catastrophe.

All creatures have an assigned place in our world, but that doesn't mean they'll stay there.

CHAPTER ELEVEN

Now

Like the watchdog she is, Tink offers to help Hope clean up the house so that she can keep an eye on her. *Alright,* Hope says with a shrug. *If you want to spend your night cleaning* . . . She doesn't know that the alternatives are long walks in the woods or a bottle of whiskey. *But no questions. In fact, it's better if we don't talk at all.*

Over the years Tink has maintained the place, but she has done nothing to prevent the thick layer of dust from forming over the furniture. Paint peels from the doors and windows. A stray cat who comes in through the hole in the basement window has brought fleas, which immediately find Hope's exposed ankles and hitch a ride.

"Ew," she says, and kicks her feet.

"White socks will do the trick," Tink says. She is leading Hope down the hallway to the kitchen, where some old vinegar and a broom lie waiting for a caring hand.

"Why, they're afraid of white?" Hope asks. Her eyes dart from her ankles to the floor, to her ankles, to the floor again.

"No," Tink says, and wonders if this counts as the talking they're not supposed to be doing, "they love it. They'll come right for you, but at least that way you can kill them one by one. Don't try to squeeze them, by the way; you have to roll them over your skin until they die, or smash them with the back of your nail."

Hope pauses. "You seem to know a lot about fleas . . . " Her nose wrinkles, which Tink thinks is cute even as she's offended by Hope's insinuations.

"I'm not the one who brought them in, if that's what you mean. Fleas prefer cats or dogs, not humans. Oh, and you'll have to vacuum daily, including all upholstery. And maybe get some diaphanous earth—"

Hope stops when they enter the kitchen. "Whoa," she says, "this place hasn't been updated in a long time."

"Try ever." Tink crouches to the level of the cabinet under the sink and removes an empty glass spray bottle and a gallon of vinegar. "Here, take this," she says, and Hope takes the supplies and carries them to the table where Tink and Peter once drank tea with the Darlings. Tink can still hear Wendy at the stove, can still see her fiddling with the ends of her apron strings.

The broom is the industrial kind, meant for scrubbing decks or debris from the sidewalk in front of a house. Many of the fibers have fallen out, like needles from a pine tree. Still, it will do for now. Tink says she will tackle the dusty furniture; Hope can sweep.

"How about you sweep," says Hope, "and I'll tackle the dusty furniture."

"Suit yourself," Tink says.

In fact, sweeping is what she intended to do all along. She thinks she understands this "Hope Darling," or at least understands the traits that they share: Don't boss her around. Don't ask questions. Don't get in her face, or she'll bite. Tink carries the broom to the front door and starts at the beginning, tracing the dry leaves and dust and needles through the house on the many paths Tink herself has made over the years.

Cleaning is for adults, Peter had repeated in Neverland so many times that it is still Tink's first thought every time she touches a bottle of Lysol. Yet when Wendy needed help making the beds, there he was, stretching the fitted sheet over a corner; when Wendy needed someone to scrub the dishes because they had no dishwasher, there he was, piling wet plates onto a linen towel spread out as a makeshift drying rack. This from a boy who wouldn't even throw out his scraps, just waited for the animals to come out at night and eat them from the Lost Boys' plates. Once, he ordered the whole set to be thrown over the falls, and then they had to use banana leaves instead.

"Hey," Hope calls out from the landing. "You've been sweeping the same spot for like twenty minutes."

"Right." Tink pushes the debris down the hallway out of Hope's sight and leans the broom against the wall. Time is a funny thing; for so many years it didn't exist for Tink, and now it's everywhere, the material with which everything around Tink is made. Peter is dead, and yet he is right here, sweeping the same floor, whistling the same Never bird song, discovering a feather probably brought in on someone's coat and tickling Tink's chin with it.

Stop, Peter! she squeals. *You know I hate when you do that.*

Do what? he asks, and the feather attacks again.

He grabs her arm and pulls her close. Tink can feel his heart beating against her back, like a hand knocking on a door. For a moment they are one organism.

Wait until I get Wendy, he says, and the moment passes. Or did it never exist at all?

"Tink! Earth to Tink!"

Hope is a soft walker, and she's taken Tink by surprise.

"What?" Tink asks loudly.

"I asked you what song you were whistling. I've never heard it before."

Tink becomes aware of her lips and stops. "I thought we said no questions."

The two girls finish their tasks. When Tink returns to the kitchen, Hope is already there, sitting in Wendy's seat. "So I changed my mind about the whole question thing," she says, as though picking up some previous conversation between them. "What have you heard about the Darlings?"

Tink puts the broom back in the space between the ice box and wall. She washes her hands. She digs through the drawer for a towel. How long can she draw this out? Peter was always the liar; Tink never cared what anyone thought enough to bother.

"I . . . Uh . . . My parents," she says. "Yeah. They told me a little bit about them. Or I guess my grandparents told my parents, who told me."

"I'm sorry for your loss," Hope says.

"What?"

"You know, your grandparents. Did you ever meet them?"

Tink turns to the cabinets and looks for a mug. She needs water. "No. They died in . . . a . . . tornado."

"A tornado?"

"That's right." Tink rolls her eyes. "We get them around here occasionally."

"I had no idea." When Tink turns around with a white porcelain mug, Hope is looking out the window, as though she expects a twister to arrive at any moment.

"Not often. Almost never. Just this one time, really, when my grandparents happened to be . . . picnicking. All they found was their basket in the school parking lot."

"That's so tragic," Hope says.

"Very," Tink agrees. She fills her mug and then rests it on the table gently, the way Wendy used to. She figures she better kill off her parents, too. "Then my mom and dad died."

"Another natural disaster?"

"Cancer," Tink says. "Well, my dad had cancer, and then my mom died from a broken heart."

"Jesus." Hope clutches at her chest. "I'm sorry."

"Thanks." Tink sips her water for as long as she can. It tastes like the inside of an old pipe.

"My mom is still alive," Hope says. "And my grandparents, too—my adopted ones, I mean. Obviously Wendy is dead, and they apparently never found out who my dad's biological father was."

"Hmm," says Tink, still sipping.

"I hate to ask, but . . . what did your grandparents say about the Darlings?"

"Mmm," Tink says. The last bit of water disappears into her mouth. "Not much. Just that there were three children—Wendy, John, and Michael—and that Mr. Darling was very ill. The children ran wild most of the time—or, not wild,

Wendy wouldn't have allowed that, but just unsupervised." *Oh no, I shouldn't have said that thing about Wendy*, Tink thinks. Even in her recollections, she can't sully Wendy's name.

"Your grandparents must have known Wendy personally then," Hope says. "Did they tell you anything else?"

"I don't think so." Tink looks up at the ceiling, as if trying to recall some detail to share. "Nope, nothing else, sorry."

"Interesting." Hope pulls something out of her pocket and lays it flat on the table. It's a picture, old and yellowed, with five children standing with their arms around each other. Under the photo, there are five names in the order of the children: Michael. Peter. Wendy. John. Tink. "Because I found this upstairs in the bedroom with the weird paintings on the walls."

Damn it, Peter, Tink rages, but it's really herself she's angry with. She should have checked the house more carefully; she should have destroyed all evidence. It's just that she never expected some stranger to come waltzing in claiming her lineage, especially not some girl with Tink's tenacity and bad attitude.

"I'm named after my grandmother," Tink says, as Hope crosses her arms. "Tink is actually a family name that goes back—"

"Spare me," Hope says. "I don't know how you're in this photo, but you're going to tell me. Otherwise, I'll be forced to call the police and tell them about a suspicious squatter in my grandmother's house, and I'm sure they won't take kindly to—"

"Fine." Tink's shoulders sag. "What do you want to know?"

"Everything," Hope says. "And start from the beginning."

PART TWO

CHAPTER TWELVE

Then

WHAT IT WOULD TAKE TO STAY a family, Tink decided that night after the children had gone to bed, was exactly the same method the Lost Boys had tried to use on her. She tiptoed downstairs to the kitchen, using only the light of the moon to guide her tiny steps, and then opened the refrigerator. Strange remnants of the Darlings' British life existed there, especially on the condiment shelf: mint sauce, brown sauce, Tewkesbury mustard.

The crisper drawers were full of produce Wendy called "kid-friendly," as though she wasn't still a kid herself: peeled carrots, chopped broccoli, grapes. These were easy to allot into plastic baggies and throw into a lunchbox like the three that took up the top shelf, from Michael's Star Wars metal box to Wendy's floral-patterned bag. John's lunchbox, true to style, was a nondescript black bag like an adult man with a boring office job would eat at his computer.

Boring bag first, Tink decided, and slid John's lunch off the shelf. Inside was a ham and cheese sandwich with no mayonnaise, a bag of baby carrots, and an apple. Tink wrinkled her nose. She suddenly yearned again for Never fruit and the way the lost boys would crack the hard shells open and let the sweet juice run down their arms. Even the "vegetables" of Neverland were better, like the bright pink Never root that the boys dug from the forest floor accompanied by scavenging rabbits of the same color from all their eating.

Michael's lunch came next. Tink suffered through another ham and cheese sandwich, but she rejoiced at the bag of gummy snacks that stuck to her teeth and left their taste on her tongue long after she'd swallowed the last bit of them. She took a bite of the apple and returned it to the tin.

When Tink unzipped Wendy's bag and removed the carefully organized contents, she did so reverently, like an archeologist lifting a newly discovered artifact from the ground. This ham sandwich was to her taste, a thick sheet of mayonnaise making the bread tangy sweet, but she only ate half. Instead of an apple, Wendy had an overripe mango. Tink bit into the skin with her fingernail and was surprised to find a sweet liquid running from the wound. When she exposed more of the orange fruit, she found the taste to be much like Never fruit—but more fibrous. Mango shreds threaded her teeth, so that later she would need to use something called "floss" for the first time.

After the lunches had been devoured, Tink dropped the bags on the floor and carried the second half of Wendy's sandwich back upstairs. She opened the door to Peter's room and waited—he did not stir. He was known to be a heavy sleeper back in Neverland, easy to prank only in the hours between sunset and sunrise, and the same seemed to be true in the real world. As quietly as she could, Tink put the sandwich under the sheets next to him.

What confusion Tink awoke to the next morning. Wendy, suspicious of her brothers first, had apparently turned their beds upside-down in search of clues as to the missing meals. Michael's pillows were on the floor of his room; John's comforter was in the hallway. All of the drawers to their desks and dressers were open. Both boys were still in their nightclothes, Michael in fuzzy pants and an oversized t-shirt and John in an old man's plaid pajamas.

"Why would I eat my own lunch?" John kept rationalizing to her. "I'm perfectly capable of throwing a slice of ham on two pieces of bread."

"It wasn't me!" Michael whined, knowing, somehow, that John was implying his younger brother might not be so proficient in his meal preparation. "I don't even like ham and cheese sandwiches!"

Wendy seemed to ignore their pleas for a while, but eventually even she had to admit neither of them were likely suspects. She looked down the hallway at Tink, but then she turned and knocked on Peter's door. "Peter," she said, knocking gently, "May I come in?"

Tink waited. She heard Wendy and Peter talking, but not what they said. Michael tried to listen at the door, but he claimed he couldn't hear anything either. Tink could barely contain her excitement. *Neverland, here we come*, she thought.

The door opened.

Wendy came out and shut the door behind her.

"Well?" Tink asked, unable to wait any longer. "Was it Peter?"

Wendy nodded gravely. In her hand was the second half of her sandwich, mushed against the plastic wrap.

"Naughty boy," Tink said with a shake of her head. "I am so sorry. This is not the first time he's—"

"—sleepwalked," Wendy said. "I know. Poor Peter was so confused when I found the sandwich under his pillow, but then he realized what had happened. We'll need a lock on the refrigerator, I think, and maybe a safer place for the knives."

She went downstairs, leaving an astounded Tink to stare after her.

When Tink went into Peter's room, she found the leader of the Lost Boys perched on his desk as though it was a branch of a Never tree. On his mouth was a satisfied smirk. "You'll have to try harder than that, my fairy friend," he said, leaping down to the floor and beaming at her. "Wendy loves me, and she won't be convinced otherwise by a little nighttime snack."

"We'll see, Peter Pan," Tink said. Her voice held a challenge never levelled at her friend before, and for a second, she saw uncertainty in his eyes. "We'll see."

CHAPTER THIRTEEN

"Legendary Pranks in the Year 1940"

Excerpt from *Neverland: A History*

JANUARY—THE LOST BOYS FILL TINK'S HOUSE with water by using moss to stop up her door and windows.

JANUARY—Tink enchants a thousand flying toads and releases them in the Home Under the Ground.

FEBRUARY—Peter Pan removes the stitches from Tink's uniform, cuts every piece two sizes too small, and re-sews the uniform.

FEBRUARY—Tink convinces the mermaids to pretend to be a sea monster using eight flexible drainage pipes for legs.

MARCH—The Lost Boys make Peter a cake, only they use crushed laughing lilies instead of flour. Peter giggles for a week whenever he speaks.

APRIL—Peter paints an enormous canvas black and hangs it around the inside of the Home Under the Ground. The Lost Boys sleep for thirty-six hours before one of them realizes what happened.

APRIL—Tink tells Peter she has to return to the fairy realm for training. While she is "gone," she hides in Peter's cabinet and moves his mug whenever he puts it down, leading Peter to glue his mug to the table out of frustration. As of the year of this book's publication, it is still there.

MAY—Peter dresses up one of the new orphans as a girl and tells Tink they've brought the wrong child back with them.

JUNE—The Lost Boys paint a ship on one side of a pair of binoculars and then tell Peter that they've spotted the Jolly Roger. When he looks through the binoculars Peter can see the ship, so for a week, he keeps watch on Marooners' Rock in case the pirates decide to come ashore.

JULY—Peter, Tink, and the Lost Boys capture a wild boar and set it loose in the Kandallanian camp. During the panic, they sneak into the Chief's house and paint a smile over his frowning portrait.

AUGUST—Three warriors from the Kandallanian camp attempt to break into the Home Under the Ground to defile something in retaliation, but the Lost Boys are expecting them and surprise the warriors by popping out of their hiding spots in unison like a hundred jack-in-the-boxes.

SEPTEMBER—Tink tells Peter and the Lost Boys that she's become engaged to a scientist from Tag and that she'll be leaving them. Then, on the day of her bridal shower, she fakes an elaborate breakup scene. It is unclear whether she ever told the boys the truth about the "Tag man" made of two Kandallanian children under a robe.

OCTOBER—Peter fakes his own death by using berries and a Kandallanian arrow, almost starting a war between the clan and the Lost Boys and ruining the peace on Neverland forever.

NOVEMBER—No pranks.

DECEMBER—Peter and Tink swap all of the Lost Boys' socks so that in the morning no one can make a proper pair. This will become the inspiration for the Lost Boys exchanging gifts of single socks on Christmas and their birthdays.

CHAPTER FOURTEEN

Now

"So you lived here with my grandmother? And a fairy boy who thought he was in love with her?" Hope twists something around and around her neck. When Tink looks closer, she recognizes Wendy's silver locket.

"Peter wasn't a fairy," Tink says distractedly, "and where did you get that necklace?"

"My father gave it to me."

Tink's hand darts forward, catching the oval piece in her palm. Like the hamsa, her hand becomes a ward against evil—though the evil, in this story, is Tink herself.

"But where did he get it?"

Hope pulls back, taking the locket with her. "He never told me. He just said it was his mother's, and that the letters engraved on the front were her initials: W.E.D."

"Wendy Elizabeth Darling."

"Right." Hope relaxes again. "So keep going. What happened after Wendy found the sandwich?"

Tink is suddenly so very, very tired. Strange that an immortal can feel fatigue, she thinks, but feelings like these keep fairies and other unearthly creatures in check. Drink too much? You won't die, but you will have a headache for days. Fly too far? You won't die, but you'll collapse in a field unable to move for long enough that an animal might come along and do the one thing that can end your immortal life—

Stop.

Don't even think it.

"After she found the sandwich . . . " Tink wants to rest her head on the table, just for a minute. If she could only close her eyes long enough to make the image of Wendy making her brothers new sandwiches and then, in the rush of catching the bus, leaving her own bag empty on the counter . . . but no. There is no amount of sleep that can wash clean the slate of Tink's conscience. "After she found the sandwiches, she and her brothers went to school. Peter played his games, and I . . . I planned my revenge."

Hope seems to think about this for a while. She is twisting her necklace again.

"I guess I'm confused. I mean, I get that you loved Peter, and he loved Wendy, and she . . . Well, how did Wendy feel about Peter?"

Even the air is heavy on Tink's skin, like she is in a grave and someone is shoveling dirt on top of her. She needs to rest. She needs to forget.

"Wendy liked him," Tink says, "but she barely knew him. Not like I did." She reads Hope's expression. "No, I don't mean that in the sense that 'I loved him more, so he should have been mine.' I mean it in the sense that even though they looked like they were the same age, Peter was a naïve little boy and Wendy was a mature young woman. She wasn't the type to believe in love at first sight."

"But they did fall in love, didn't they?" Hope asked eagerly.

"Love—" Tink repeats. The word is the shovel pounding the final layer of dirt down. "—is never as simple as that."

Perhaps Hope needs a break from Tink's story; perhaps she has finally realized that Tink cannot go on. Her wheels are spinning in the mud of her past. The sky has grown dark as they've sat there, becoming the dusk that used to mean *It's flying weather.* The birds tweet out their last call. Tink wants to pull the dark sky over herself like a blanket, to turn over and close her eyes and never wake up again.

"Come on," Hope says, her voice kinder than it's been all day. She puts out her hand. "Why don't you rest for a while, and then we can finish the story tomorrow."

Tink places her child-sized hand in Hope's five long fingers and allows Hope to lead her upstairs. Tink expects to stay in her old room, but how would Hope know which one was hers? "Not that one," Tink says when Hope pauses in front of the Neverland mural, but she accepts John's room, library that it is.

"Let me know if you need anything," Hope says, as if she is the host of the house and Tink the guest. Earlier this would have bristled Tink's wings—just an expression, now—but she's too tired to care. *Make yourself at home,* she thinks. *This place will only bring you pain.*

A minute later, she is asleep between John's dusty sheets.

* * *

WHEN SHE WAKES UP, MORE SNOW has rendered the window into a wall of white. For a second, she forgets where she is—and when she is.

After she remembers Hope and the untold story from the day before, Tink finds an old debate team t-shirt in John's top drawer and changes into the stiff cotton. Wendy used to iron all of their clothes, even their shirts. *You're not their maid,* Tink used to remind her from her perch on the washer. *I know,* Wendy said, *but it's just my way of . . . expressing myself.*

Love again, Tink thought as Wendy bent down to the mouth of the dryer. *Making work for all of us.*

Tink has never looked carefully at the books on John's shelf, but she does so now. Her eyes scan several histories of various parts of the world, math textbooks, anatomy. She stops at a book that has a worn spine and takes it down to investigate. Shakespeare again, she thinks, and rolls her eyes. Yet when she turns the pages, she finds that in the margins are not notes on the text but John's own thoughts, quick jolts of emotion he showed no sign of at the time.

There is a boy called Peter Pan, who makes me feel—

Tink turns the page.

He only has eyes for Wendy, and yet—

Tink slams the book closed. Apparently, she was not the only one with passion burning unrequited in her breast. *Your pain is your own,* she thinks, and returns the book to the shelf. She wonders what happened to John—did he find his own version of Peter to love him back? Or was he still alone, like Tink, forever in love with her ghosts?

When she goes downstairs, the kitchen shows signs of use: a dirty pan with a ring of dried egg, a white mug with a chip like a missing tooth, a cup that holds less than an ounce of forgotten juice. There is a plate covered in a lid, which, when Tink explores further, turns out to be her own breakfast. Scrambled egg, toast, an individual clear dish with a pat of butter inside. *This Hope girl is making it harder to dislike her,* Tink thinks as she wolfs down the food without bothering to sit.

Tink finally finds Hope where she least expects her: outside. Through the window she spots the black coat, a red hat with a ball of red fur on the end, and two bare legs with their feet slipped into a pair of the boys' old dress shoes. Hope is just standing there, looking up slightly, with her arms out of view.

"What are you doing?" Tink asks when she opens the door a crack.

"Watching the snow," Hope says.

She doesn't turn around or come back inside, so Tink puts on her own coat—more of a jacket really, she admits now that her arms are shaking—and boots and joins her in the yard. Hope's arms are stretched out, like an orphan asking for food, and snowflakes are falling into her cupped palms and melting there, falling and melting, becoming just a drop of water on the frozen earth.

"Haven't you seen snow before?" Tink asks.

"No," Hope says. "I mean, not before yesterday. I'm from Ft. Lauderdale, and it never snows there."

"Hm," says Tink by way of response.

"Have you been there?" Hope asks.

Tink shakes her head no. "I used to go everywhere with Peter, and since he . . . you know . . . I've gone nowhere. I've never even left this town."

Through Hope's eyes, the snow seems miraculous. Tink can still remember the first time she and Peter had a snowball fight with the Darlings, and the way they had immediately run for cover as soon as the leader of the Lost Boys bent to scoop a fistful of snow. Peter had been best at throwing the balls of snow and ice, but Tink had been stealthier, waiting for him to gleefully deplete his stock and then showering him with all of her ammunition. How the Darlings had cheered—even Wendy—and how Peter had pouted, snow melting down his head like a cracked egg.

Later, Mr. Darling had made a surprise appearance—his last, though they didn't know it at the time. He came downstairs in a blue terrycloth robe and corduroy slippers with the backs bent down from years of sliding feet, and his face was bearded and very gray. "Father," Wendy had said, as if reminding him, and the strange man had sat in a worn armchair by the fire and waited while his children gathered around his feet.

"Will you tell us one of your stories?" Michael asked. His hands petted his father's slippers.

"Yes, please," John agreed. Wendy said nothing; she knew better than to hope.

"Very well," Mr. Darling whispered through lips that barely moved. "Your mother and I met on a day just like today. Cold. Snowy. She was visiting from England, and her aunt's house happened to be right next to mine. The first time I saw her, she had her hair in two long pigtails, and there were little snowflakes in the braids. Do you know what she was doing?"

"Making a snowman!" Michael shouted. Apparently, he had heard this story before.

"That's right. She was picking up handfuls of snow and patting it onto an enormous white ball—the first of three, I surmised, and so I stopped to help her. She didn't seem to notice me, but she did put my ball on top for the snowman's head. And do you remember what she said right before I left her that day?"

"*We've given him life. Now it's our job to protect him.*"

"Very good, John. She was much like Wendy, fiercely loyal even to a lifeless tower of snow." Mr. Darling looked at Wendy and then away, as though staring directly at her face brought him pain. Tink understood the feeling. "She guarded that man with her life every morning and afternoon when the other children walked home from school, and if anyone got too close, she would . . . " Mr. Darling succumbed to his dry cough, the one that always carried down the hall during the night when Tink left her door open. " . . . she would chase them off with an armada of snowballs. I became her devoted soldier, and I . . . added . . . what muscle I could to the operation, even though it earned me . . . a black eye from Bobby Hann. What did I care about a black eye, in the matter of true love?"

Here he stopped and coughed, and coughed, until Wendy rose to pour him some tea from the kettle already warming on the stove. Up to his room he went, after a pat on the head of every child in the room including Peter and Tink. A week later, he was dead.

* * *

"You should leave," Hope says.

"What?"

"I said, 'You should leave.'" Hope finally puts her hands, raw and red from the cold, in her pockets. "What's so great about upstate New York?"

"You're here," Tink says. Then she stutters, "I didn't mean 'You're here' like that was a reason I was here; I meant 'You're here' as in 'If upstate New York is so bad, why are you standing here right now?'"

"I know what you meant." Hope laughs, and the sound echoes through the empty yard. Even the birds have found branches to perch on, and the squirrels are safe in their caves and dens. Then her mouth turns down. "I'm here because I needed to know the truth. And because my dad died last year, and I never got around to asking him."

"Shit. Sorry, I didn't know . . . And that story about Mr. Darling . . . "

"No, it's fine. As you said, you didn't know."

Tink tries to shake some warmth into her fingers, to blow on them, to slide them into her tight jean pockets. It has been a long time since she's just stood outside, with no sidewalk to dig or grave to dust or bottle of liquor to sip. Come to think of it, she has a flask in her coat pocket, which she removes and sips.

"Want some?" she asks Hope.

"Sure."

Hope takes a small sip and coughs. "What is this?"

"Whiskey."

"It's terrible." Hope takes another sip. "You know, my dad used to drink whiskey sometimes. Never in front of me, but I'd find the empty glasses on the porch table and smell them. Mom drinks *rosé*, and only from a long-stemmed glass."

Tink doesn't say anything.

"They were a weird match. Mom's really gone off the deep end now that he's dead—doing things like dying her hair purple and buying a Lexus even though there was nothing wrong with the Honda dad got her. She's dating a bartender named Brian, who looks like he should be teaching rich tourists how to surf. It's like she wants to pretend Dad was never here or something."

Tink takes back the flask and finishes the rest in a big gulp.

"It must be weird looking like a kid but feeling like an adult," Hope says. "I get so mad at my mom when she treats me like I'm five years old, but you . . . You're on another level."

"Tell me about it. I feel like I've been alive for an eternity, but I still can't get a decent drink."

The two girls turn back toward the house, as though in silent agreement, and walk up the porch to the door. They both stomp their feet to kick off the snow, then step inside and remove their boots. Hope suggests they sit in the "green room," which is a small formal room off of the dining room, and Tink agrees with a shrug.

"This was Mrs. Darling's room," Tink says as they enter. "No one ever went in here."

The room has the stamp of a woman on it, like a kiss at the bottom of a letter. Floral armchairs, bouquets of silk flowers, a glass bowl in the shape of three leaves connected at the stems that probably once held little candies with raspberry filling. Tink likes this room, not because of the decorations but because this room holds no memories. Wendy and Peter's ghosts do not enter here, though they're waiting by the threshold. Once the two of them are seated, Tink facing the window so she can look out on the white blanket of the backyard, she takes the offensive position.

"What did your dad know about his parents?" she asks.

"I've told you almost everything. He had the locket, and there was a short letter with him when he was given up. It said, 'This is Andrew. He likes milk and being held. His parents are dead. If he ever wants to know more about his parents, he can find them in Briar Bend Cemetery.'"

"I never was good at writing," Tink says.

"*You* wrote that letter?"

"Sort of. I dictated it to the nurse who cared for Wendy. She's the one who helped me with the paperwork, and the arrangements for Andrew."

"And did you tell Wendy's brothers about my dad?"

Tink looks down at the coaster on the wooden end table next to her chair. The cork is covered by a white laminate printed with leaves that match the glass dish, like a little sprig of mistletoe. Peter would have held it over her head and instructed her to kiss him, which she wouldn't have, and then he would never have let her live it down.

"No," she says. "I told them the baby was dead."

"Why?" Hope asks. She doesn't seem mad, but then again, this is not her life. She is once removed from the chaos of Wendy's death, an audience member in the symphony of Tink's past.

"Because that's what Wendy wanted." Tink shakes her flask and then remembers it's empty.

Tomorrow, she will bring two.

CHAPTER FIFTEEN

Then

After the sandwiches came John's homework folded into paper airplanes and flown across the yard; Michael's favorite teddy bear, Mr. Jackson, blinded and stuck through the spike on top of the weather vane; Wendy's nightgowns cut into pieces and sewn back together as a quilt. These pranks of Tink's were all the more believable as the work of naughty Peter because Peter himself made so many mistakes. He mixed the peanut butter and jelly together and then left the sticky mess in the cabinet, where it bred fruit flies. He ripped out pages from Mr. Darling's books, thinking that the instructional on identifying mushrooms in the forest was meant to be removed from *The Pocket Guide to Edible Wildlife* because why else would the word "pocket" be in the title? John, who had helped Peter find the right book in the first place, was especially distraught over the book's destruction.

"Naughty Boy," they called him, coopting Tink's name. Still, everyone loved Peter.

Wendy was especially patient with the Lost Boy, sitting him down every time he made a mistake and explaining, in a mother's voice, what he had done wrong. This nurturing only increased Peter's affection, so that he talked, when the children were at school, about marrying Wendy one day. "What about Neverland?" Tink would ask, and Peter would shrug helplessly, as though he had no control over the matter.

His chance to make his move came in early November, when the leaves had disappeared from the trees and the brisk morning air promised snow. Wendy had just put a baked ham in the center of the table when there was a knock from the other side of the house. "Who would come by at this hour?" she mused, and all of the children had raced down the hallway to the door to find out. Peter, the fastest of all of them, got there first, with Tink close on his heels and the rest not far behind. There, holding a bouquet of grocery store flowers in yellow plastic, was a young man with broad shoulders and a blue blazer that fit well up top but went down to his knuckles. His dad's, Tink thought, and then noticed the father in question waiting in a car in the driveway.

"Hi Paul," John said, seeming to know the boy.

"Hi John," Paul said. He looked down at the flowers. "Hi Wendy."

"Hi Paul. How are you?"

Paul seemed to consider this question for a long time—or he forgot Wendy had asked it. He scuffed his foot against the welcome mat in front of the door and then said, "Do you want to go to the Winter Ball with me?"

"Oh." Wendy clasped her hands together, like a nun in prayer. John's eyebrows went so high they disappeared under his bangs, which had fallen from the swoop of his school comb over. Michael bounced with manic energy. Tink eyed Peter without turning her head and noticed the shade of his cheeks, which had turned a jealous crimson.

"Who even are you?" Peter demanded suddenly.

"I'm Paul," said Paul.

"Don't be rude, Peter," Wendy said sharply, and whatever Peter's next question was going to be, he didn't ask it. Still, he did what he could, which was cross his arms and glare. "Paul," Wendy said now, turning to her suitor, "I thought you had a crush on Mary from down the street."

"Mary?" Paul asked, glancing up and to the right. "Mary who?"

Wendy smiled kindly. "Mary who you asked to the movies last Friday."

"Oh. That Mary." Paul was still kicking, but this time with his other foot. "She said no."

"And you were going to ask her to the Winter Ball at the movies, but since she didn't seem interested, you thought you'd ask me instead?" Wendy asked.

"I guess that's right," said Paul. His flowers were dangling from his hands, and he kept tapping them against his right leg.

"Oh Paul," Wendy said, "I'm flattered, I really am. But I happen to know that Mary only said no to the movies because her father doesn't let her go out with boys, not because she doesn't like you. In fact, she told me just yesterday that she was afraid she put you off and that she hoped you'd still ask her to the ball because her dad was going to make an exception to his rule for just that night."

"Really?" Up went the flowers. Silent went Paul's feet. "You mean it?"

"I do. But why don't you ask your dad to drive you over to Mary's house right now and ask her yourself?"

"Thanks, Wendy!" Paul said. He practically ran down the stairs, and a minute later, the headlights of his father's car had disappeared from view.

The boys went back into the house, ignorant to the feelings of Wendy, who sat down on the front step and crossed her arms over her knees.

"That was nice of you," Tink said as she sat down next to her. "Really nice. I don't know a lot of girls who would give up a date to a dance for a friend."

"Mary isn't a friend," Wendy said, "I barely know her. But it was the right thing to do. And besides . . . I didn't want to go with Paul or any other boy who's in love with another girl. I want to go with someone who likes me, or with no one at all. I'm not afraid of being alone."

"You don't have to be alone," Tink said. "There are lots of people who like you."

The girls sat there on the porch for a while, listening to the creatures burrowing and creeping and stalking in the darkness. A fox slid into the light from the porch and then back out, becoming just another shadow in a shadow world.

"Tell me about where you're from," said Wendy. Tink had the feeling that she was sad, but not about the dance.

"Alright." Tink searched her memory for a detail she could share, just one small thing that wouldn't sound ludicrous to a girl in Wendy's position. "Back where I'm from, the trees are the most wonderful trees you've ever seen. They're taller than any tree here in America, and have twice as many branches, and are perfect for climbing no matter how grown you are. All of the leaves are in the shape of hearts, and when you pick a leaf and give it to someone, it means you like them."

"You're giving them your heart," Wendy said softly. "I like that." She seemed to be studying Tink, her expression as intent as when she had read Shakespeare. What lines were written on her face, Tink wondered, and what lines were folded up like a note and buried where Wendy couldn't find them?

Tink had always found the leaf tradition silly—only little boys would come up with such a way of expressing their feelings—and yet she had bristled when Tiger Lily had given Peter a leaf after he rescued her at Marooners' Rock. Tink needn't have worried, since Peter had later dropped the leaf into the bonfire, but now she wondered if it was an inability to love that had made him so insensitive, or if it was just an inability to love anyone but the right person. There had also been the incident with her own leaf offering . . . but she preferred not to dwell on that.

"Look." Wendy bent down further and then came up with a leaf from the step below her feet. The leaf, perfectly shaped as a heart, was recently fallen and therefore red and unblemished.

"It's the perfect one."

Back in Neverland, the boys had mostly used the leaves as fuel for their bonfires. Now, Tink felt like the single leaf in Wendy's hand, blades boldly waving in the breeze, was brighter than any flame. Were the words in her heart showing on her face? Was that why Wendy kept staring at her?

Wendy held the leaf by the stem and then lifted it to Tink. "Here. You can have it."

Tink stared at the leaf. Her cheeks burned, and she found she could not move, not even her lips to make a joke or her fingers to take the offering so carelessly given. Perhaps Wendy, a girl of the real world, had not understood the gravity of what Tink had said about their tradition. Perhaps she had understood exactly.

Wendy moved closer.

Tink's hand rose.

"There you are!" said John's voice behind them, and Wendy dropped the leaf. Tink moved to catch it, but the red heart disappeared into the darkness beyond the porch light and was gone. "Peter has a surprise for you."

Michael, who had come to fetch Wendy too, took his older sister by the hand and led her inside. Tink, following behind them, mused on what had just occurred. Could Wendy . . . ? And could Tink . . . ? Was it possible? And what would Peter say? And how would they—

Peter stood in the middle of the living room surrounded by piles upon piles of leaves. When Wendy entered the room, he scooped up two handfuls and released them up into the air, where they caught a little wind and drifted slowly down on top of Wendy's head.

"Peter!" Wendy exclaimed. "You've made a mess of the house!"

But she was laughing, and the boys too. Silly Peter, naughty Peter, fun Peter. Tink scowled. Peter took two more fistfuls of leaves and presented them to Wendy, who put out her hands and let the leaves rain down onto her palms and then the floor.

Perhaps Wendy had not understood . . .

Perhaps she had understood exactly.

"Go to the Winter Ball with me?" Peter asked.

"Oh Peter," Wendy said. "I would, but—"

"No buts," Peter said. "No excuses. Look, I've even gotten you a dress!"

Michael ran to the closet and returned holding a long plastic bag that trailed on the floor behind him. Inside the bag, flattened and wrinkled, was a gaudy pink dress with puffy sleeves and a lace collar. Tink wrinkled her nose.

"Oh Peter," Wendy said again, but she was laughing. "I can't wear something like that!"

Peter took the bag from Michael and threw it behind him, where it billowed to the floor and was trampled by Michael's excited feet. "I don't care if you wear a trash bag," Peter said, "but you'll go with me, won't you? Please say you will, Wendy, or I'll be ever so sad."

"I . . . I . . . "

"Please, Wendy?" said little Michael.

"Alright, you win. I will," she said. She didn't look at Tink, hadn't made eye contact with her since they came inside.

"Hurray!" The boys whooped and danced around Wendy, throwing leaves in the air and letting them fall on her head. She laughed and caught some of the leaves, releasing them again so that they showered on the heads of the boys.

* * *

THE NEXT MORNING, TINK FOUND THE eldest Darling at work in the kitchen with Nana, like a Christmas tree skirt, curved around her feet. No one else was within hearing distance, so Tink grabbed a piece of buttered toast off the pile and asked, between bites, "So . . . you and Peter . . . the dance . . . "

"Right." Wendy washed a plate, her hands like two carp leaping. Tink wondered if the tips of her fingers were pruney, or whether they were as soft as the skin of her arms where Tink had touched her that morning while they made breakfast. "It'll be fun."

"Of course it will," Tink said. She picked up a tea towel, but there was nothing to dry. "Peter always has fun."

Wendy was still washing the plate, or rather, rewashing it, and the bubbles covered her hands like a layer of foam on a pond. "There's more to him than that," she said softly.

"Oh really?" Tink's voice was louder. "Because you're such an expert on Peter Pan? You know him *so well*?"

"I know he's more than you give him credit for," Wendy said.

Tink snorted. The tea towel had become a twisted thing in her hands. "I give him exactly the credit he's earned. I could tell you stories . . . " But here she stopped. Tink dropped her left hand, allowing the tea towel to spiral into a long tail, and threw it on the counter. "Never mind. Whatever he is, you'll find out for yourself soon enough."

"Tink, it's just a dance—"

"I'm going to my cottage," Tink said as she crossed the kitchen. "I don't want to be disturbed."

"Tink—"

But she was already at the door to the backyard, slamming it.

The sound of a plate breaking against a metal basin echoed behind her.

CHAPTER SIXTEEN

"Peter Pan"

Excerpt from *Neverland: A History*

Some readers might wonder how Peter Pan became the leader of the Lost Boys. Of course he was the first rescue, most familiar with the terrain of Neverland and favorite to Princess Fern, who handpicked him from several orphans abandoned during her trip to Earth, but the headship of a group like those rascally children is not won easily, even by an eldest boy.

As it turned out, Peter had many natural talents. He was an excellent swordsman, a skilled climber of trees, and a keen lookout for the dangers that might befall young boys living unmonitored on a wild island. He was the best at imitating voices; the best at negotiating with the Kandallanians, and charming the mermaids; the best at, frankly, everything. Had he stayed in the real world and been kept by his mother, he might have become Prime Minister one day.

So why did his mother leave such a charming, intelligent redheaded baby alone in a carriage in Kensington Gardens?

Several in-depth studies have been written about the topic, but their conclusions are only speculative. Peter's mother was extremely wealthy and, though unmarried, had the resources through her maternal line to care for such a child. Some researchers suspect that it was her life on the stage that called to her, drowning out the cries of her seven-day-old baby. Some researchers claim that Peter Pan's father was a married man, and that his red hair might have given away his paternity. Whatever the reason, when Princess Fern happened upon the round-faced cherub with the impish smile and dimple in his left cheek, she bent down to lift him to her own breast and whispered, "I have just the place for you."

Of course, the matter of Neverland hadn't been settled, and it was the Fairy Queen, not Princess Fern, who could allot fairy land to people seeking asylum. Thus, Princess Fern took little Peter home with her and kept him, like a pet, in a box under her bed. Her maids were apprised of the newcomer and given orders to feed him only the purest sap from the tree. Now we know that babies cannot actually live on sap, but luckily for Peter the immortality spell kept him from wasting away during the three weeks it took to convince the Queen to settle the Neverland matter.

It is said by those who worked closely with the baby that he never seemed frightened of the winged creatures bringing him sap and changing his soiled clothes, and he never emitted a single cry.

I was lucky enough to be assigned a post on Neverland during the transition period discussed in the chapter on "Flora and Fauna." The Queen called us Keepers, but really, we were glorified babysitters. Still, we enjoyed our part in the founding of that new land, and as new babies were added to the throng and began to follow baby Peter around the Home Under the Ground, we watched as Peter began to take his place as leader of the Lost Boys.

That name, by the way, was one of my own making. It came not from the fact that the boys had been "lost" by their parents, but from the fact that we spent most of our early days on Neverland in long games of Hide and Seek. Peter was the best hider, and sometimes it would take us three days to find him perched at the top of a Never tree.

"Oh well," I would say with a shrug when the game was up. "I guess Peter has become one of the Lost Boys."

"I'm not lost!" he would yell as he swung down from a hidden branch on which he had been feasting on Never fruit.

It would not be until the Darling period that Peter truly earned his name.

CHAPTER SEVENTEEN

Now

"I JUST DON'T UNDERSTAND," SAYS HOPE. "Why would Wendy hide the baby from her brothers?"

Tink arches her eyebrows. "Why do you think?"

Hope plays with the tassel on one of the chair's decorated arm covers as she seems to think about her own question turned back on her. "Because she didn't want them to have the kind of responsibility she had?"

"Bingo."

The silence after this confirmation leaves Tink alone with the memories of Wendy that often come to her at night in separate images: brown hair on a starched white hospital pillow. Faded blue gown that was never tied closed. Beep, beep, beep. Wendy's hand on the sheet, dry and cold as a corpse. Her whisper, coming from unmoving lips, cracked like a desert survivor: *Does he live?*

He lives. Tink leaned in, her ear just an inch from Wendy's mouth, and felt the cool breath of someone leaving our world. *He needs you, Wendy.*

No. Wendy might have been smiling, but whether at Tink or someplace calling to her from the other side, Tink didn't know. *Andrew's yours now, Tink. Find him a good home, away from the boys, so that they can all grow up happy.*

But Wendy—

Promise me?

I—

Tink never got the chance to promise. Still, she fulfilled Wendy's wishes, and then she stood between John and Michael and held their hands at the funeral and helped them contact a great-aunt who was retired and could come care for two boys she barely knew. Only then, when the boys had begun to play again, had she disappeared. Now Tink thinks of John, Professor of Classics at Yale, and little Michael, football coach for a team called the Bulls—or maybe it was the Danes?—smiling at her from the library's computer the only time she'd gone inside the old brick building. What use did she have for books? Even though she had learned to read, words still seemed like ants crawling over the pages of the tomes in John's room.

"My father did have a happy childhood," Hope says.

Tink shakes herself into the present. "Good," she says, once she knows when she is, "I always wondered."

Hope looks at her hard. "You never checked on him?"

Tink doesn't reply.

"Come on, Tink. Admit it. My grandparents told me that dad used to have an imaginary friend he called his Fairy Princess, and that he claimed it was this fairy, and not him, who made mischief around the house when they went out. One time, she even left a cigarette burning. Even though she got him into trouble, when she stopped coming, Dad was apparently distraught. Tried to run away to find his Fairy Princess so often that Grandma and Grandpa had to get locks put on his window to keep him in."

"So I checked on him." Tink puts her feet up on the glass table in front of her. "And I stirred the pot a little. So what? Andrew was such a little adult—he needed to loosen up and have fun."

"I knew it! But why'd you stop visiting him?"

Tink looks at her feet. "Because he grew up."

How to explain this divide to someone who has only lived in the world of men? For Tink, there were only two sets of people: children and grown-ups. To the first, she was dedicated, their warrior guardian; to the second, she was just a shadow, always just out of their sight. To do otherwise was to tempt fate, for though fairies were immortal, there were still ways to destroy them, and these adults were always the ones to deal the blows.

"Sort of." Hope smiles. "But there was always a part of him that loved to play. When I was a little girl, he turned our whole basement into an intricate miniature town, with a train that circled through the buildings and under the mountains and back through the buildings again. There was a movie theater, and a courthouse, and even a grocery store with miniature food on the shelves."

"He got that from his father," Tink says.

"But he had Wendy's serious side too." Hope's smile disappears. "He was a really good dad."

It only now occurs to Tink that there is somewhere Hope should be. It is early December, when kids of Hope's age are taking finals, or returning home to see whether their parents have turned their bedrooms into home gyms.

"Does your mother know you're here?" Tink asks.

Hope goes back to playing with the pillow tassels, which is the only answer Tink needs.

"You should call her."

"Why?" Hope's voice has lost all of its nostalgia. She seems angry, and though Tink knows she should drop the subject, she can't. She is the guardian of children, always.

"Because she's probably worried about you."

"Doubtful. Brian is probably getting her a piña colada at the tiki bar in Cabo as we speak. I still can't believe they went to Mexico for Christmas, as if I was just supposed to . . . " Hope trails off. "Anyway, I don't think she even knows I'm gone."

Christmas.

Of course.

That is why the lights in town look extra bright from her cottage window—twinkling through the trees like fireflies in the woods behind the Darling house.

"I have an idea," Tink says. Though she knows she might regret it, she tells Hope to put on her boots and coat and meet her outside in ten minutes.

* * *

When Tink returns to the Darling house, she is disguised in a large wool hat that covers her ears and hair. She wears sunglasses, even though the day has already turned dark from the clouds carrying the impending snow, and three sweaters under her coat to add extra bulk.

"You look ridiculous," Hope says when she sees her. "Like a kid who just went through her mom's closet. All you need is some smeared red lipstick."

"I'm in disguise because I don't want anyone in town to recognize me," Tink says, as though that should be obvious. Then she looks Hope up and down, noting Wendy's old red coat and boots that used to be John's. "What's your excuse?"

"No warm clothes." Hope shrugs. "I came here right from Atlanta. The black coat isn't even mine—I borrowed it from a friend from Boston."

Like two orphans—and in a way, they are both orphans, or at least strays—Tink and Hope set out down the road that led to Briar Bend. Though most houses were empty, the residents at school or work, Tink feels the eyes of her neighbors boring through her disguise all the same. The ones who know of her existence call her The Little Guardian, thinking, as was natural for people of their class, that she is a helper hired by John and Michael to care for the Darling house in their absence. They never see Tink up close, and thus they can't tell that she hasn't aged. Besides, the stoop of her back against the wind and snow is that of a much older woman.

As they get closer to town, the trees thin and then disappear. The road becomes smooth, the lines bright white from a recent painting. The sounds change, from birds and squirrels to the bustle of cars and people parading up and down the strip. By the time they turn onto Main Street, they are both shivering. Immediately, Tink feels the bustle pressing on her chest like a weight. There is too much noise. There are too many eyes. Even the word OPEN, flashed in red neon in every window, seems like an attack.

Hope, on the other hand, seems the happiest she's been amidst the storefronts and old-fashioned ice cream shops currently selling candied nuts and fudge through the winter. When offered a chunk of salted caramel from a teenager in an apron and puffy coat, she puts her hand out and accepts the sample instead of pushing forward, as Tink would have done. Her eyes find the lights strung above her, pearl necklaces on the beautiful bare throat of the sky, and stay there so long that Tink has to yell "Coming through!" at an old woman with a walker shuffling in Hope's path. The Christmas tree also draws special attention, and Hope insists that they find a place on one of the town square's benches and enjoy the view.

"Amazing how they can take a perfectly good tree and ruin it," Tink complains.

"You didn't have Christmas trees in Neverland?" asks Hope. Her body is pressed to Tink's side, though Tink doubts there is much warmth passing between them.

"Every day was Christmas in Neverland," Tink says. "But we didn't use glass balls and fragile white snowflakes. Everything that adorned a Never tree was from the forest: acorns, colorful leaves, dried berries strung on blades of straw."

"Well, I like this one," says Hope. Then she leans over and spots the ice-skating rink, empty now that school is in session. "Should we . . . ?"

"Absolutely not," says Tink.

Five minutes later, she finds herself strapped into a pair of blades. They are laced so tightly that her feet go numb—or maybe that is the cold conquering her extremities. She finds skating makes her clumsy, and that she has to hold onto the wall just to remain upright.

"Come on, Tink!" Hope is graceful as she slides down the rink, makes a loose curve, and circles back to the struggling fairy. "Aren't you supposed to be graceful?"

Tink thinks of her wings, spread out in soaring splendor. She thinks of the flipping contests she and Peter used to hold, when they would spin spin spin until one of them threw up.

"I guess not." She would cross her arms, but she can't let go of the wall.

Hope doesn't seem to tire of gliding the length of the rink, which Tink likens to a hamster wheel. Tink gets the hang of the long stride eventually, and stopping requires so much effort—and pain, in times when she has to crash into the wall—that she follows Hope's pointless circles.

It is at this moment in her newfound mastery that a little boy of about three years old runs into the rink. He wears little red mittens, and his shoes are also red and untied. His mother calls his name from the side—Peter—and tells him that he can't be on the ice without the proper shoes. Little Peter exclaims, "Look Mom!" His arms go wide and he slides sideways, putting him directly in Tink's path. "I'm flying!"

Tink knows that she is going to hit the boy. She is certain of it, and yet she is powerless to stop herself. Her feet tilt back, but instead of slowing her down, this trips her so that she clown-walks toward little Peter with her own arms flailing wildly.

Wings, give me flight, she thinks, and makes the wish without even realizing it.

Like a skydiver releasing a parachute, Tink wrenches back as her wings appear and make enough air resistance to stop her. The little boy ducks, but Tink's wings guide her left and then stop her in the middle of the rink, looking, to the few shoppers who have stopped to watch her slow progress, like her shoulders have been pulled by invisible hands. A guardian angel, they think, the Christmas tree toppers fresh in their minds.

"Thank you, thank you," repeats Peter's mother. She is on the ice now, enveloping her son in a hen-like hug, dragging him away from the girls. Tink shakes her head no, she did nothing, she is no savior, please, there is no need to thank her for anything. Her arms are shaking. She feels weak. The back of the mother's brown coat makes her look like a bear leading her cub away from a frozen lake's danger.

"You almost killed that kid," Hope says when she skates back to Tink. She doesn't seem to realize how shaken Tink is, and her eyes keep darting up.

"I think it's time for me to go back," Tink says. She is ashamed. She needs her wings off now. She cannot bear the temptation of them, like a voice in her head whispering that Neverland is just a short flight away.

"Okay," says Hope. Then her eyes go up again. "Where have you been hiding those wings?"

CHAPTER EIGHTEEN

Then

When Tink returned to the Darling house the next morning, resolved to pretend that nothing had happened, she found all of the children out on the lawn. The morning was brisk, so they wore bulky wool sweaters Wendy had likely knitted for them—all except for Peter, who was attired in a terry cloth robe and a black top hat with a worn rim. John had Wendy pulled close to him and seemed to be showing Peter and Michael something.

"What'd I miss?" Tink asked. Already she had begun to question her resolution, but she couldn't leave Peter—not after everything they had been through. She was his guardian, and if she left him there in the real world, he would never return to Neverland.

"John is teaching Peter how to dance," Michael explained.

Tink snorted. "Peter Pan? Dance?"

"I'm a great dancer!" Peter said.

"Of course you are," Tink said, "if by 'dance' you mean leap around a fire shouting obscenities. But if you mean dancing in the traditional sense, then no, you are not a 'great dancer.' You're not even a mediocre dancer."

"I'll show you!" Peter said.

He grabbed Wendy's hand and yanked her away from John, who had been muttering something to Wendy about *1-2-3 1-2-3*. "Come on Wendy, follow me," Peter urged, and he began to parade her around the yard, every step to a different tempo. First he rocked Wendy one way, then drastically the other way, like a ship on a rough sea.

"Try to stay on the beat," John shouted. He began clapping his hands in an effort to force some kind of rhythm on the prancing pair. "Careful of your partner! Watch her feet!"

Peter's own feet seemed determined to leap despite his best intentions, and he tapped his way back with Wendy trying to keep up the pace.

"Stay grounded!" John urged. "Think sashay, not *pas de chat*!"

When Peter spun her without warning, Wendy was wrenched like a dandelion spore spinning in the wind. "Faster!" Peter urged, using his free hand to speed up her pace, until poor Wendy collapsed on the grass, a freed marionette grateful for its severed strings.

"Peter Pan, you are such a show-off," Wendy said through gasps.

Peter went as stiff as the trunk of a Never tree. Wendy's eyes watered, and everyone, even Michael, averted their eyes. "Perhaps we should try again tomorrow," John whispered, and in a rare act of awareness, he patted Wendy's shoulder. Peter's chin sunk into his chest, and then his whole back curved, making him look suddenly like the old man Tink imagined he would become if she didn't rescue him.

"Wait." Tink walked over to Wendy and put her hand out. Wendy smiled gratefully and took it, her chilly fingers gripped in a grateful squeeze. Once Wendy was unfelled, Tink let go of her hand and turned to Peter. "Peter Pan, may I have this dance?"

Peter raised his eyebrows. "Really?"

"Oh shut up and take my hand, you clown."

Peter took her hand, and Tink led him to the center of the yard. "Give us a beat," Tink instructed, and John began his low *1-2-3, 1-2-3*. "Pretend that you're a reed swaying in the water at the edge of Mermaids' Lagoon," she said in Peter's ear, so that no one else could hear her. Then she stepped left, and Peter followed her.

Tink had never danced the way of mortal men before, but fairies have natural grace. She relied on the balance her wings afforded her, and they did not let her down. When Peter drew closer to her, she could feel his warm chest and, inside, his rapidly beating heart. The flush that had come with Wendy's scolding had paled into Peter's normal glow, the glow of a child who finds everything fun and amusing for the novelty of it.

"Why is it so much easier with you?" Peter whispered.

"Because you're like a river," Tink said, "always dancing and forging its own path. Before, with Wendy, you were trying to stop your flow. Instead, you lost control." She used his hand to spin herself around. Then, abruptly, she stopped moving and looked him in the eyes. "A river can't be stopped, Peter Pan. It can only be redirected."

"Bravo!" exclaimed John, unaware of the conversation happening between his two pupils. "Just like I showed you. Now Peter, why don't you try those same moves with Wendy?"

* * *

WHEN JOHN AND MICHAEL CAME INSIDE, flushed from their dancing, Wendy and Peter were not with them.

"You should have seen them," John said through a mouth full of peanut butter sandwich. "It was like night and day. They were . . . they were . . . "

"Extraordinary," finished Michael with a sigh.

"Where are they now?" Tink tried to act like she didn't care that much.

"Not sure," said John, still caught up in his educational accomplishments. "Probably still practicing that last move I showed them, the double reverse spin."

Tink went out to the yard, but only the tracks in the leaves betrayed Peter and Wendy's presence. Where could they have gone? Some of the leaves seemed to be disturbed in the direction of the road to town, so Tink followed the rough lines of shuffled leaves to the main path and then over it, to the woods on the other side, where the tracks picked up again.

If Tink had been a bloodhound, she would have gotten on all fours and sniffed the earth. As a fairy, she had only the tracks and the broken twigs of the trees to guide her. The air was getting colder, and she wondered if it would snow soon. In her hurry to find Wendy and Peter, she had left the house in only the long-sleeved shirt donated to her by John. *Mathletes '18*. Tink pulled the sleeves of the shirt closed with her fingers, hopeful that she might block at least some of the air chilling her hands. The tips of her wings quaked against her legs.

"Peter!"

Wendy's voice drifted from somewhere to Tink's left. She slowed her steps, hoping not to be discovered. There appeared to be a grove of pine trees past the oaks, and these were dense and almost impenetrable. Tink ducked her head into her arm and pushed through, like wading through a waterfall, but slowly, so that she might peer through the needles without betraying herself.

"Wendy."

Tink fought the urge to roll her eyes. Had these two really snuck out into the forest to repeat each other's name over and over again? *Peter, meet Wendy. Wendy, meet Peter. Great, now that that's covered, can we go home?* But even as she ranted to them in her head, Tink knew there was more going on beyond the boughs. As her face emerged into empty space and she stopped with the rest of her body covered by branches of needles, she already knew what she would find. She braced herself against it, or tried to, and yet when she saw the two bodies clutched like fish schooling, she was not prepared. She realized she would fall, and then she fell. All she could do was direct herself backward, out of the pines, onto the cushion of dead leaves that turned her thump into a whispered whoosh.

"What was that?" asked a breathy voice.

"Probably just a nosey bird," said a second, and this one belonged to Peter.

Tink thought of Wendy, prone on the ground, one hand on Peter's back and the other on the skin of Peter's neck exposed by the short sweater collar. Then she forced the image away. She could not go on, remembering it. She could not fulfill her duty. *This never happened,* she told herself, but when the wind rained little green needles onto her face and she closed her eyes, the image returned.

With nothing else to do, Tink rolled over, stood up, brushed the leaves off of her shirt and wings, and walked home.

CHAPTER NINETEEN

"Fairy Anatomy"

Excerpt from *Neverland: A History*

FOR THOSE WHO HAVE NEVER SEEN a pair of fairy wings or heard of their usefulness, I must stop here and offer some general information:

Fairies stand about four feet tall on average, though some fairies have measured at three feet two inches and one fairy, Tall Legs, hit a whopping five feet. Their wings are usually exactly as wide as their height, and can support the small-boned creatures by ligaments at their backs. The most common color is green, but there can be variation in the shade and sparkle. Typical wing speed is twenty beats per second for soaring, and one hundred beats per second for rapid flight.

A fairy's wings make her fly, but they also function as balancers, temperature regulators, fairy dust makers, and mood stabilizers. That last one bears further explanation, especially as it relates to Tinker Bell and her state during her time on Earth, so I will briefly go through the process of a fairy's system.

Fairies enjoy sap from their tree, but the only sustenance they actually require is air. From that air—which they both breathe and beat through their wings—they draw out water, oxygen, and a secret element that humans cannot detect called Pixium. When Pixium enters the thin membrane of a fairy's wings, it is strained and dried into a fine powder—or "dust"—that settles on the wings.

That "fairy dust" is known for its ability to let humans fly, but its true function is the regulation of a fairy's mood.

Occasionally, a fairy is born who has trouble reabsorbing the Pixium from her wings. Fairies like this one are often ill-tempered, and even sometimes go so far as to break the sacred rules that obligate the rest of the fairy realm to good behavior. In Tinker Bell's case, she had both the trouble with reabsorption and then, later, stopped producing Pixium altogether when she removed her wings.

One might say that the first problem led to the second . . . but we will save that judgment for a later chapter.

CHAPTER TWENTY

Now

"You can see them?" Tink asks.

"They're hard to miss."

The girls look up at Tink's wings, much like a butterfly's only longer, the tips like two enormous bunny ears far above Tink's head. They are green, like the uniform Tink should be wearing, with shimmers of white, yellow, and blue depending on the way the light hits the gossamer material. In the cold air they wave back and forth, sails against a frigid wind, until Tink orders them to swing downward and back, the way a fly settles its wings when it lands.

"Must be Peter's blood in you," Tink says. "He could always see my wings—there was a kind of innocent belief in him."

Tink and Hope leave the rink and return their skates, not saying much in the meantime. It has snowed a little since they came into town, and their old footsteps are now imprints that crunch flat under their feet. Even the forest seems to understand the gravity of the situation. Tink fights the urge to rip her wings off now, as if they are a scab that she wants to run a fingernail over. She hates the way they drag behind her in the snow like one long beaver tail. She hates the way she wants to love them. *You don't deserve to fly*, she tells herself—as if she needs reminding.

"Are the stories about fairies true?" Hope asks. Her voice is startling after being silent for so long.

"Which ones? Fairies have gotten quite a reputation over the years."

"Let me be more specific." Hope stops and grabs Tink's arm. "Can you sprinkle your dust on a human and make them fly?"

Tink looks down, but then she catches sight of her wings and looks up again. "It's true," she says. She is too tired to lie.

"Can you take me?"

"I don't fly anymore." Tink turns to go, but Hope stops her.

"Please?"

There is something in Hope's desperate look that reminds Tink so much of her fallen friends. She has Wendy's sensible brown eyes, but the wideness, the wonder of them, is all Peter Pan. If he saw something new, nothing could stop him from investigating it—even if that thing were a venomous snake, or a volcano spitting lava, or a sailor with a hook for a hand.

"Here." Tink runs her pointer finger over her right wing and it comes away covered in glitter. She then rubs her thumb and pointer together over Hope's shoulders, since she can't reach her head. "You don't have to think pleasant thoughts, but it doesn't hurt."

As soon as the dust hits Hope, she floats off of the

ground a few inches. "I'm flying!" she exclaims, as if what she's doing is anything close to what Peter and Tink used to do. Her legs frog kick, bringing her a few feet higher, and then she's through the leaves and up in the sky.

"Stay close to the trees," Tink calls upward. "Don't let anyone see you. Make sure you're on the ground in five minutes—not a second more."

Then, without telling Hope where she's going, she continues on her trek.

* * *

TINK DOESN'T HAVE ENOUGH ACID LEFT to remove her wings. She stole the compound a long time ago, and the laboratory has since put up security cameras that even crafty Tink can't evade. Even now, she dilutes the acid in order to make it last longer, making the process slower and therefore more painful. Currently, there is less than an inch left in the bottle, with one spare bottle in the bathroom.

She looks around her cottage for something else she can use—A butcher knife? A pair of sheers?—and her eyes move out the window, to the stump where she chops wood on the occasional night when she allows herself the luxury of warmth.

You can do this, Tink. You have to.

The position is an awkward one. Tink must sit on her knees in the snow, twist her neck and back to the left in order to lie her wings on the stump, and then swing the axe around her back with her right hand. She is pretty sure she can aim true—but not one hundred percent sure. If she misses, she might get a shoulder, or worse, a spine instead.

So what? she thinks. *Worst case, you put yourself out of your misery.*

Tink takes a deep breath. The axe is heavy in her hand, and she swings it a few times to practice. Her arm barely extends far enough, and her shoulder is already sore from the difficult motion.

On three. One, two—

"Stop."

The axe is above Tink's head. Her eyes dart around the clearing, expecting to see Hope, but there is no one there.

"Who said th—"

"Me," the voice says again.

Peter. She would know that arrogant claim anywhere.

"You're not real," Tink says.

"So what?" he says. "My shadow wasn't real, and yet somehow I ended up chasing it on all kinds of adventures."

"That's different," says Tink.

"Sure it is. But at least it distracted you long enough to put that axe down."

Tink looks at the axe lying on the ground beside her.

"Come on, Tink," the voice urges. All of his mocking humor is gone. "It's time you came home."

"I am home." And she means it. Even before the accident, this cottage was all she had.

"Come on, Tink," the voice says again. "We both know where you really belong."

"You always were sticking your nose where it didn't—"

"—Come on!" Peter interrupts, "Come on, come on, cuh-caw!"

Tink realizes that she is talking to a blackbird perched on a nearby branch. Cuh-caw, it says again, cuh-caw, cuh-caw!

Great. Now I'm going crazy.

But she doesn't pick up the axe. Her wings stick straight up in the air, sensing a change in the wind.

Damn you, Peter, she thinks.

In one graceful move, Tink pushes off of the ground and flies.

CHAPTER TWENTY-ONE

Then

THE NIGHT AFTER THE INCIDENT IN the forest, Tink couldn't sleep. Every time she closed her eyes, she saw Peter and Wendy in the pine grove, felt the sting of needles on her wings when she fell, fought the nausea that comes with knowing you have witnessed something you can never unsee—yet somehow, she needed to, for Peter's sake and her own. She remembered the bottles in Mr. Darling's liquor cabinet, and though she had never tasted the amber whiskey or clear vodka, she suspected that they worked much like the wine the Kandallanians made from Never fruit.

Since their arrival in New York, the nights had gotten colder and colder. Now, Tink's breath led her like a ghost, through the trees and across the lawn to the Darling mansion. A light snow crunched under her boots. Wendy had left the porch lights on again—Tink wondered if she did this for her but had never asked—and when Tink reached the circle of light, she dragged her tired feet across the mat and then ditched her shoes by the door.

The house was quiet, so Tink tiptoed down the hallway to the living room, where embers from a fire glowed stubbornly in the fireplace and reflected over a dozing Nana's coat. Tink couldn't help pausing to warm her hands, which were chilled and slightly chapped. Wendy had cleaned the room since whatever revelry she and the boys made, but left up a sheet strung up between four dining room chairs, which served as a fort much like the Lost Boys made during their overnight adventures in the Never forest. *Oh, what adventures the Darlings have learned from Peter,* Tink thought, and then she felt incredibly guilty for plotting to separate them, so she forced the thought away.

Mr. Darling's liquor cabinet was on the far side of the room, near the glass door that led to the back porch. The Darlings never sat out there, and Tink wondered if perhaps the single rocking chair on that side of the house had been Mr. Darling's preferred thinking spot before his illness. Strange how places become sacred that way, like shrines to the living. Now she bent down and blew a little fairy dust on the lock, causing the top half to spring open in an attempt at flight, and removed the first bottle she found.

Glasses adorned the shelves on the top half of the cabinet. Tink was not sure why there were so many styles, but she decided the smallest one would be easiest to hide and filled it to the brim. Like a thimble, she thought, though really the glass was several times as large. She also noticed a silver lighter engraved with roses, and this she slipped into her pocket without knowing why. Maybe it reminded her of the roses that lined the Fairy Queen's castle; maybe it reminded her of the way she had once engraved metal with the same artistic skill.

Thanks for everything, Mr. Darling, Tink thought, and swallowed the liquor in one gulp.

The taste was terrible. Perhaps the drink had gone bad, though more likely this was just another example of how adults tortured themselves into being miserable. Jobs were another, and dates, and bills, and really most things that made up an adult's glum existence. Tink locked the cabinet back up and replaced the glass, hoping none of the children would notice the sticky yellow film on the inside or the missing lighter.

"What are you doing?"

Tink whipped around and found Wendy standing in the doorway in a pink nightgown with small roses along the neckline. Had she seen Tink drink? Or worse, had she seen her take the lighter?

"Sorry, I didn't realize I wasn't welcome here anymore," Tink shot back.

This seemed to sufficiently confuse Wendy. "I didn't mean that," she stuttered. "Of course you can come in anytime, I just meant . . . well . . . Do you need anything?"

"No." Tink's panic subsided. Wendy wouldn't notice the missing drink, or the used glass, or anything Tink did. In fact, she seemed more distracted than normal, and Tink wondered if the events in the woods had anything to do with it. "Do *you* need anything?"

Wendy smiled faintly. "No one's asked me that in a long time. But no, I'm fine. I just come down here to listen to music when I can't sleep. If you want, you could stay for a few minutes and listen with me?"

Tink shrugged as though she didn't care one way or another, when in reality, she was more than happy to delay returning to her lonely cabin for a few more minutes. The only thing that waited for her there was a cold bed—and the nightmares that would come to her while she slept in it.

Wendy bent down on her knees and rubbed a finger over the spine of what looked like flattened cardboard boxes. Eventually she found what she was looking for and drew one of the items off of the shelf. When she flipped the case over, a shiny, flat black object slid out.

"What is it?" asked Tink.

Wendy looked at her strangely. "It's a record. You've never seen a record before?"

"Oh. I have. That one just looks . . . different."

Wendy evaluated the record, seeming to look for the difference that Tink saw. "Maybe you're thinking of a 45?"

"Probably. That sounds familiar."

Wendy went over to the small table on the other side of the glass door, where a strange machine Tink had never noticed before sat. She flipped up a plastic cover, revealing another round, black disc—this one attached to the machine—and a long black arm. She placed the record on the disc, lifted the arm, and placed it on the outside of the record. The record spun, and music began to play from the speakers.

"Amazing," said Tink. She was thinking that this sounded better than any of the terrible music John and Michael played from their TV speakers.

"It's Bach's 'Prelude Number One in C Major.'" Wendy sat in a wooden armchair and sunk into the cushioned back. She seemed too world-weary for a child—but then again, maybe she wasn't a child anymore. "My mom used to listen to this exact record every night before she went to sleep, and as she tucked us in she would hum it in our ears. This necklace," she held up a locket around her neck, "used to tickle my cheek as she sang in my ear."

Tink shifted her focus from the quality of the sound to the music itself. She knew enough about human music to recognize a violin, though they didn't have string instruments in the fairy realm and found them unappealing in the human one. Like screeching cats, Godmother Anne used to say, as though her guards knew what a cat sounded like.

Whatever it was, this music, drifting up and down, around and around, was pleasing to Tink's ear. She closed her eyes and let her mind wander; she came upon an image of Wendy spinning in a field of flowers, kicking up spores of dandelions like fairy dust floating through the air. Smiling like she was smiling now, remembering like she was remembering now, in a world where Mrs. Darling was still alive and Wendy was still a child and Peter and Tink had never come upon their search party that night in the woods.

Tink opened her eyes. She was surprised to feel a tear slide down her cheek.

"I'm sorry that you grew up," Tink said before she could catch herself.

Wendy opened her eyes. "I'm not. Growing up is a beautiful thing, Tink. Think about if we only ever had seeds and no flowers, or saplings and no trees to climb."

Tink wanted to tell her that in the fairy realm there were flowers and trees too, but without the darkness of death hovering on the horizon. Instead, she closed her eyes again.

"How about you?" Wendy asked. "Does your mother ever play you anything?"

Tink thought about Godmother Anne, who was the closest thing to a mother Tink had ever had. "No," she said, "but where we live has its own rhythm. I guess you could even call it music."

The record finished, and the room went silent.

"What does it sound like?" Wendy whispered.

Tink hadn't thought about the fairy realm in a long time—or rather, she had thought about it all the time, but in the sense of her duty to the crown and her worry that Godmother Anne would discover Peter's absence. Now, she tried to think back to a lazy afternoon after one of her last days as a tinker, when she had wandered out of the town center to the outskirts on one of the long branches that ended a few feet before the dangling leaves that divided them from the rest of the magical realm. She had sat down at the edge, back to the royal castle and the homes that clustered around its base, and closed her eyes in much the same way she had during Wendy's song. Soon she would be up in that castle, then sent away to some distant place that Godmother Anne called Neverland.

"It sounds like leaves rustling in the wind," Tink said. "But that's just the sound on top of all of the other sounds. If you listen closely, you can hear an undercurrent of water below the ground, and voices bartering in town, and the wings of . . . birds . . . flapping so fast that they become a bee-like buzz. The whole town just hums, and you're one part of it, humming yourself." She looked at Wendy. "Does that sound crazy?"

"It sounds beautiful." Wendy smiled. "Everything is always so quiet here. I like the idea of a constant hum. It's . . . comforting."

Tink went over to the record player and fiddled with the dial Wendy had spun to turn it on until the little red light went off. Then, without turning around again, she began to hum Mrs. Darling's song. She didn't remember all of the notes, but fairies have notoriously beautiful singing voices, and she knew that the song would sound sweet even if she missed one or two. As she sang, she thought back to that time on the branch, and Bach played over the whisper of the willow.

"What are you singing?" a new voice said over her humming. She knew, without turning around, that Peter was the one who had interrupted her.

"It's just a little something I heard somewhere," Tink said. She turned around to find Peter in a pair of John's pajamas. He looked ridiculous, like a toddler who has stepped into his father's shoes. His eyes went to Wendy, who wiped away tears, and then to Tink, who tried to turn her face as stony as a statue. Still, Peter knew her too well, knew her flat mouth and too-focused eyes and red cheeks, and even a carefree boy like him could sense when he had interrupted a moment between two people.

"Well it's a silly song," he said, "and some of us are trying to sleep." Then he turned to Wendy. "Aren't you coming back to bed?"

"In a minute, Peter," she said. Her voice had a hardness Tink had never heard before, and Tink knew that Peter had made a grave mistake. "Tink and I are in the middle of something."

After Peter went away—he even stomped his way up, audible to Tink's precise hearing much farther than Wendy's—Wendy came over to Tink and took her hand. To Tink's surprise, she lifted the back of Tink's hand to her mouth and kissed it with her warm lips.

"Thank you," Wendy whispered. "It really felt like she was here."

Before Tink could say anything or even move, Wendy followed Peter upstairs.

CHAPTER TWENTY-TWO

Godmother Anne's Introduction to "Mothers"

Excerpt from *Neverland: A History*

THOSE CAREFUL READERS KEEPING SCORE MAY have noticed that the role of mother has featured heavily in many of my previous chapters. What, you may be wondering, is so special about a mother?

I have many theories about why this person—or persons, in the case of some of the subjects of this book—have become so important. Firstly, many of the people I've discussed either lost their mothers at a young age or never had a mother to begin with. Peter was abandoned, as were the Lost Boys; the Darlings' mother was dead; Tink never had a mother to begin with. A rare case, Hope Bain actually had a mother, but for a time that mother, Mrs. Bain, fell short of the expectations her child had of her.

Still, my original question remains: What is so special about a mother? Why did these children, these motherless babies-turned-adolescents, retain such a strong yearning for someone they either never met or had lost permanently?

The answer, I believe, lies in the role the humans created for the women of their society. Take, as a counterexample, the Fairy Realm. Here, we are all expected to be feminine, and flirt, and flit; we are also, on the other hand, expected to play all parts to our growing empire. All of the guards are women. All of the craftspeople are women. The fairies who cook your breakfast are women, but so are the fairies who consume that breakfast and then go off to secure the border against an invading army.

In the Fairy Realm, women are ALL.

On Earth, however, women have traditionally played a much different role—one that has, in its description, the part of caretaker. Women are expected to become mothers; as mothers, they are to do the labor of the house—not just cook and clean, but check homework and monitor behavior and kiss bruises. Women are HALF of the parental unit, yet like an egg when cracked down the center, their part in the labor of the house is never an even split. Someone must get the yolk.

Take, for example, Wendy Darling. Only a few years older than John, she almost singlehandedly ran the Darling house until her untimely accident. The only person to help, for the brief period of time she stayed with them, was Tink.

Of course, Wendy had other motherly roles to play as well—but I'm getting ahead of myself.

CHAPTER TWENTY-THREE

Now

THE AIR IS COLD AND DAMP, and Tink shivers with every strain of her wings. Still, there is a warmth in her heart that keeps her moving. Her guilt tries to overpower the heat—*Think of the children you've hurt, Tink. List them. Wendy, Peter, Andrew, John, Michael*—but at least temporarily, their names fade away again. They are like stars hidden behind the clouds, and when the wind shifts, they will reemerge brighter than ever.

For now, she is free.

She veers left and circles the woods. Hope is not anywhere in sight, and Tink imagines her floating somewhere above the rink like a hot air balloon. Humans are not skilled fliers—with the exception of Peter, who flew like he was half fairy himself—and she will not get the hang of the currents and breezes before the fairy dust wears off.

Tink still remembers the first time she took Peter flying. He was younger then, maybe eight years old, and even leaner than most children that age because he lived off of the land. When you move from walking to running to swinging from Never trees to building treehouses from their branches, you become as strong and slim as a wild animal. She had given him fairy dust before, allowed him to float up through the trees and back down again, but at thirteen he seemed ready to take on the responsibility of flight.

"Now Peter," she said in a firm voice. She looked into his curious eyes and then away, because she was tempted to laugh and flying was a serious matter. Back then he was just like a brother to her, or a very demanding pet. She did not see humans as anything like herself. "When you get to the edge of Neverland, you'll know it by the line that divides the sparkling purple atmosphere from the blackness of the in-between space. Straight on takes you to Earth, though you're not ready to go back there yet; left takes you to the fairy realm, though of course humans are forbidden from entering there. Right is the giant lands, though you're not permitted—"

"Well, where can I go?" Peter interrupted. His arms were twitching. He was anxious to get started, Tink knew, but she was stalling. Something about setting Peter loose on the human world terrified her; who knew what was waiting for him on the other side?

"You can fly around Neverland for starters," she said, "and be grateful the fairies have granted you this privilege at all."

Peter bent his head, properly chastised. Tink knew she had this power over him, like placing a saddle on a giant squirrel—and that someday, like those magnificent creatures inevitably did, he would find a way to escape her. No one in the fairy realm knew what happened to their oversized creatures; some suspected they had tunneled under the willow tree, while others claimed they stored up fairy dust somewhere and then used it to fly away. Tink liked to imagine them endlessly summersaulting through space, emitting their squirrelish squeaks. She did not, however, like to imagine Peter doing the same, and she knew she'd have to watch him carefully.

"Can we please fly now?" Peter asked. He put his hands out, a pauper begging for a coin.

"Very well." Tink bent one wing and sprinkled fairy dust into his hands in a careful allotment of three shakes. Two circles around Neverland and he'd be out of juice. "Throw that over your head and push off."

Peter did as he was told. Though Tink did not know it then, the twinkling flecks falling on his head looked like snow falling on the Darling's front lawn. Peter rolled from his heels to his toes and stretched his neck and head as high as he could; gradually, he lifted off the ground and floated away.

Now, as Tink circles the town and then shoots off toward Niagara Falls, she thinks of the way Peter whooped and laughed with every jolt and soar. He was so happy, and though back then she had taken flying for granted, now, she understands his joy.

Wait.

What was that?

A shadow behind one of the nearby clouds reveals wings, a thick body, a helmeted head. Could it be Godmother Anne? Tink has seen signs of her guardian over the years—a full cup emptied of coffee and sparkling with dust; a trail of pixie powder down the walkway to Peter and Wendy's graves—but Anne has never spoken to Tink nor revealed herself before.

"Godmother Anne?" Tink says loudly, though the wind swallows the sounds.

The wings and head come closer, closer, and then burst out of the cloud, revealing a bald eagle that screeches in surprise when it sees what it probably thinks is a flying human. Tink is startled too, and she loses her balance and tumbles out of the clouds into the clear air. Luckily she is somewhere wooded, and she hopes there are no campers or birders aiming their binoculars in her direction. She quickly regains her stability and returns to the misty covering, where she searches out her companion.

The bird is gone—just like Godmother Anne.

Tink hasn't seen a sign in over ten years, not even the faint shimmer of a speck of dust on her carpet that could be a shard left over from a broken glass. She wonders, every few months, what happened to her, and whether she got in trouble for Tink's insubordination.

More likely, she has grown tired of Tink's monotonous days, her coffee mornings and grave afternoons and drunk nights, and has gone home. More likely, she has forgotten all about Tink—a reversal, for once, since usually it's the children who forget. Not that Godmother Anne was actually Tink's mother—or rather, not in the traditional sense—yet Tink sometimes thinks of her that way, even as she simultaneously considers herself an orphan. Both mothered and motherless.

After Tink met Godmother Anne at her stall, the next time she saw her future guardian was during her interview. According to the Council seated around the Queen's table—the Queen herself was absent—they had found her questionnaire . . . concerning.

"We fear you haven't taken this opportunity seriously," said a fairy with dark black hair decorated by glossy bees that had been dipped in some kind of plastic coating. Tink wondered how she had gotten the bees, and whether they had been dead before their preservation. In the Fairy Realm, they tried to use all parts of the land provided to them by the willow tree . . . but was wearing dead insects really a useful method of recycling?

"Listen," Tink said, and then she sat down at the empty seat at the table. She had been too anxious to sleep the night before, and now she was tired and grumpy. "I take this position very seriously, but I'm not going to pretend to be someone I'm not just to get it. *You* picked *me*, a simple tinker, for reasons that I hope will be explained soon, and if I'm falling short of your expectations, you only have yourselves to blame."

"Myself?" said a voice behind Tink. "But I've only just arrived."

Tink turned around slowly, knowing before she even set eyes on the crown of shimmering moths that circled the head of the Queen that Her Majesty would be standing there.

"Your Majesty, I—"

"Please," the Queen said, walking past the chair where Tink sat—the *royal* chair, she realized, only now noting the engraved moths on the arms—and taking a rest on the edge of the table, "do elaborate on what you see as my shortcomings."

The Council's eyes were bug-wide, and Tink herself had forgotten to blink the whole time the Queen had been talking. She did so now, several times in succession, and then said, in a more controlled tone, "Well, Your Majesty, I just meant . . . I was trying to say . . . "

Godmother Anne put her head in her hands, as though already anticipating whatever Tink was going to say.

"Well, if I'm being honest, I think it's rude of the Council to pull a craftswoman from her work and ask her to interview for a job without telling her what that job is, especially since not completing that duty, should it be assigned to that craftswoman, would be treason." This last sentence came out so quickly that Tink had to gasp for breath afterward.

"Rude?" mused the Queen. "I can't agree with your word choice, but your point is understood." She looked at Godmother Anne, who was now watching the Queen through her fingers. "I see why you chose her."

"See, that's what I mean," said Tink. "Everyone keeps telling me I'm perfect for some position that I don't even—"

"Enough," said the Queen. Her voice had lost its whimsy, and her bemused smile had disappeared. "Your point has been heard and considered, and I will remind you that it's more than a common fairy deserves from this esteemed Council." After a pause, the Queen's face softened back into whimsy. "As to your post, I will do Godmother Anne the honor of detailing it—and Tinker Bell, I shall leave the choice of duty or treason to you."

The Queen had smiled then, and the Council had followed her lead, though they didn't seem to understand the joke. Tink understood it perfectly, but did not find her current position nearly as amusing as her monarch did. When she and Godmother Anne were out of the castle, the older fairy had pulled Tinker Bell into an alley and scolded her for over thirty minutes about how much trouble she could have caused. *You have a great future ahead of you,* Godmother Anne had reminded Tink. *Why derail the train before it's even left the station?*

Unfortunately for Godmother Anne, this reproach had the opposite effect of what she intended.

Firstly, Tink didn't know what a train was, and she certainly didn't know how it related to this so-called "station." Instead of understanding the metaphor, which she would only connect much later in life, she focused on the first half of the reprimand—the part about her *great future.* What did the Council have in mind for her?

Secondly, and more importantly, Tink had never felt so loved.

* * *

Now, as she flies, Tink tries not to think of what Godmother Anne thought about the accident, and yet the not-thinking leads to thinking, as it always does. Did she blame Tink? Was she angry? When she told the Queen, did she cast her eyes down the way a mother would when explaining away her child's wrongdoings? Was Tink banished from the fairy realm, as many disobedient fairies were? No one had ever alerted her to the fact . . . but then again, she had never tried to go back.

And I never will, she resolves again, though the repetition is unnecessary.

Fairies always keep their promises.

CHAPTER TWENTY-FOUR

Then

THE NEXT MORNING, TINK FOUND THE Darlings in the kitchen in a flurry of activity. As she stepped over the threshold, she heard an unlikely splash under her boots, and she realized that the sink had sprung a leak. Michael and John were skating around with towels under their feet—mostly spreading the water, Tink noted—while Wendy and Peter argued. Peter lay on his back with his head under the sink and his feet sticking out to the table, and water kept spraying into his eyes and mouth. Wendy was crouched down next to him, talking in a louder voice than Tink had ever heard her use. A damp Nana had retreated to dryer ground under the table.

"That's not it, Peter, I'm telling you. When father used to—"

"I know, I know, your father was apparently a hundred times more capable than silly old Peter."

"That's not what I'm saying—"

"Maybe if you said less, I might actually be able to focus on fixing this leak."

Wendy closed her mouth, and it looked like she was actually biting back her words. By her feet, a rusty toolbox had been emptied, or rather ransacked, for the wrench Peter held in one hand. Tink bent down to watch him work for a minute, and, realizing he had no idea what he was doing, announced in a firm voice, "I'll fix it."

"Oh great," said Peter, who was now out of view, "good old Tink has joined the peanut gallery. Do you want to tell me about how your father used to fix the sink, Tink, or should I just—"

"Damn your ego, Peter," Tink said. "You're wasting time and ruining their floor." This was a tone of voice she didn't often use on Peter, and a second later, he wiggled out of the cabinet and stood up. His cheeks were pink, and though she knew she'd embarrassed him—*Good,* she thought—she didn't do anything to soften the blow.

Tink searched through the tools on the floor for a second wrench. Once she had the instrument in-hand, she took Peter's place in the sink cabinet and lifted the second wrench with her other hand. The trick, she knew, was to tighten the compression with one wrench while holding the valve with the other.

The water stopped.

* * *

THAT AFTERNOON, PETER ANNOUNCED THAT HE would be taking the boys on a surprise "field trip."

"Me too?" asked Michael, who always seemed afraid of being left out since he was so much younger than the others.

"Especially you," Peter said. He bent down on one knee to look into Michael's eyes, but Tink noted that his glance strayed to Wendy. He was putting on a show for her, the way he used to fly circles around Tiger Lily's head. "You're an important member of our crew."

Peter wouldn't say where the three of them were going, only that they needed to wear warm clothes and bring their father's toolbox—the one Tink had just used on the sink. *Not obvious at all,* Tink thought. She had seen this show many times, especially when one of the other Lost Boys proved to be more skilled at anything than Peter.

Think you can shoot an apple off of Little Ben's head?

Peter will blindfold himself and aim—and you'll be the target.

Think you can best Peter at swords?

Peter will blindfold himself and fight—and you'll be on the other end of the sword.

Never mind that these battles always ended in a scraped knee or a black eye or once, during an especially dangerous game of "who can hold his breath the longest," the loss of a life. Tink had been back in the fairy realm that time reporting to the Queen on the most recent Kandallanian birthing ritual, and when she'd returned, she'd found a grave dug at the edge of the Home Under the Ground and over it, on a stick, the letter L.

"We wanted to bury him proper," Little Ben had said when he saw her staring at the grave. "But by the time we finished covering him up, we couldn't remember his name."

Lance, she'd thought, and taken off her hat. *His name was Lance.*

That time, Peter had disappeared from the Home Under the Ground for five whole days. Tink had searched the island for him, and then, on day five, found him up in a Never tree scraping the bark off of a stick with a knife the way humans peel apples. She didn't ask him where he'd been until then; even boys deserved to have their own private spaces. When he'd been ready, he'd made himself available to be found—as she'd known he would.

"I killed him," he said as soon as she alighted on a nearby branch.

"Who?" Tink asked. She knew, but did Peter?

"Him. The boy with the lazy eye." Peter peeled more quickly. Tink wondered whether he would accidentally slice his finger, and whether he wanted to. "I challenged him, and he didn't back down."

Peter continued to scrape, only the stick had fallen out of his hand, so the knife moved through the air like it was a conducting wand.

"It was an accident," Tink said.

Peter didn't say anything. He had found another stick and was peeling, peeling, peeling away. She was surprised he still remembered the contest at all—Lost Boys usually forgot things within a day or two—and she wondered if there was something about the stick, about the repetition of this action, that kept Peter's memory? Was he infusing it with his thoughts the way a praying believer might send their worries into a string of beads?

It didn't matter. No human mind was stronger than the spell.

"He didn't back down," Peter said again. He sounded less sure this time. Were his memories changing color the way the stick was? Would he soon whittle away his worries entirely?

"Can I borrow your knife?" Tink asked.

"My . . . ?" Peter looked down at his hands as though they weren't attached to him. He blinked. Whatever mantra he'd been repeating had been interrupted. "Oh. Um. I guess. But make sure you give it back."

"I will," Tink said, and took the knife by the hilt.

As soon as the weight of the knife shifted to her, Peter smiled.

* * *

"What do you think they're doing?" Wendy asked from her chair. She and Tink were waiting on the porch. The day had come and gone, and still, the boys had not returned. That day had been their first chance to be alone for longer than a few minutes, and Tink had hoped to spend the day with the eldest Darling; unfortunately, Wendy had seemed too distracted to care, even before the darkness had fallen. She had spent the day in her room, only emerging to slowly chew two pieces of toast with marmalade and later, in the afternoon, for a cup of tea. Was she worried about her relationship with Peter? Was she angry? Tink didn't know, but she suspected that much like Neverland, the paradise of their relationship had begun to show its darker side. Even now, Wendy kept sitting up, tapping her feet and then collapsing back into the chair.

"I don't need to think," Tink said. "I know."

"You do?" Wendy stopped fidgeting. "What are they doing?"

"What Peter does best," Tink said. "They're building a treehouse."

Wendy laughed at first, but then she must have realized Tink was serious. "A treehouse? Really?"

Tink shrugged. "That's Peter for you."

Still, the boys did not come. Even for Peter, keeping children out in the cold was careless, and Tink began to worry. Wendy resumed her tapping, and Tink couldn't help her own feet twitching in time. When 9 p.m. came and went, she proclaimed, "I'm going to look for him."

"But Peter said—"

"I don't care what he said." Tink stood up and shook her limbs until they warmed. Then she turned to Wendy and put her hand out. "Well, are you coming?"

Wendy took her hand, and her palm was surprisingly warm despite the cold. Tink thought back to the night before—the first time they'd touched—and wondered when unrelated incidents like this one became a trend. Come to think of it, Tink had never seen Peter and Wendy hold hands; when they went anywhere, Peter always rushed ahead, while Wendy stayed behind to herd the rest of the group.

Now, Wendy took a flashlight out of her coat pocket and aimed it ahead of them. Leave it to Wendy to always carry the right supplies, Tink thought—one of the things she most admired about her. The circle of light illuminated a footstep, and though Wendy stopped to try to analyze the print, Tink pulled her along. She was an excellent tracker—an unusual skill for a fairy, whose main responsibilities included flitting—but she didn't need to apply her skills to the hunt. Peter was predictable, and a few days ago he had pointed to a tree on the far-left side of the Darling property and said, with admiration, "Now there's a good treehouse tree." He would be there, she knew, hammering and nailing the old beams stacked in the Darling's backyard from a previous unfinished project until he felt satisfied that he had outdone Tink's simple plumbing, and the next day, he would bring Wendy out to admire his hard work.

Sure enough, as they neared the tree, their footsteps were accompanied by loud banging. John came into view first, since he was asleep against the tree's trunk. His mouth was open, and a string of drool ran onto his scarf. Peter had probably exhausted the boys by making them carry the beams back and forth; they didn't, after all, possess any of the necessary building skills.

Wendy tilted the light up, revealing Peter dangling from an unnatural angle in order to hammer in another beam. In just a short amount of time, Peter had completed the base and two walls; the third would be done within the hour. When he put up the fourth, she knew, he would sing his wall song—*Four walls, four walls, steady and strong, four walls*—and do a little jig.

I need to convince him to take up a new hobby, Tink realized.

"Where's Michael?" Tink called up.

The hammering stopped, and then Peter slid down the rope like he'd slid down the sail of the Jolly Roger. "Pretty great, isn't it?" he asked Wendy, slightly out of breath. He hadn't heard Tink, or had chosen to ignore her. "When I'm done, we can have little picnics out here, or even spend the night."

"Where's Michael?" Wendy asked.

Peter looked around. John had finally begun to stir at the sound of their voices, and he now stretched his arms wide and then looked down to his right where, Tink realized with a sinking feeling, Michael should have been sleeping too.

"When was the last time you saw him?" Tink asked. Her voice was too loud; she was angry for Wendy's sake. Peter had been in charge of the Darlings, and in just a few hours he'd lost one.

"I guess it was . . . Well, he went to get some small sticks for the . . . Or maybe it was after I . . . " Peter looked at John.

"An hour ago, maybe less."

Tink got down on all fours and felt the ground for prints. Her fingers found the grooves of a shoe pointing toward the end of the property line—the side that led to a creek—and then she took off running. Peter called after her, but she didn't turn around—she didn't even hesitate.

It felt good to move, and she used her wings to urge herself farther, faster, in big bounds. Branches whipped at her cheeks, stung, maybe even drew blood. A thorny vine found her coat and held on, until she tore the whole string of leaves away from the plant. She was fast. She was the wind itself. Her wings itched to fly her up out of the trees, but she knew that down below she would have a better chance at finding clues. *Soon,* she promised.

Michael had broken sticks and branches too, and she followed the smaller trail of destruction down a path, toward the whisper of water. There were other signs of the boy now—the smell of the Darling shampoo, a lost glove—and then there, on a rock in the center of the creek, Michael himself. He was hunched over, hugging his knees with one arm, and the second arm dangled unnaturally by his side.

"Michael?" Tink called out.

"Tink?" Michael turned his head without moving the rest of his body, and Tink saw that his clothes were soaked and he was shivering. Poor thing couldn't lose a minute of heat, even to greet his savior.

"I'm coming," she said, though from a quick evaluation of the surroundings, crossing the creek would be more difficult than she'd first assessed. Melted snow had flooded the usually small waterway. There were several other rocks, but none of them were close enough to Michael's to leap. Tink dropped a leaf in the water to check the strength of the current, and the green boat sailed away and was lost on the horizon before she could count. The water seemed to laugh at her attempt.

Think, Tink, she scolded. *How did Michael get over there, then?*

She looked up. Ahead of Michael's boulder, a tree branch was like a wooden beam from which the boy had been hung and dropped. The tree branch had snapped—hence Michael's fall—but it would take her most of the way. She followed the branch back to her side of the creek and identified the tree the branch belonged to. Judging by the sticks bundled and hauled up to that very same branch, poor Michael had been trying to construct a treehouse on what any skilled treehouse builder would have identified as a poor foundation. No wonder the branch had snapped and thrown Michael into the water.

First, Tink removed her shoes and socks. Then she laced her fingers behind the trunk and leaned back in order to prop her feet lower down and wrap them, as best as she was able, around the trunk with the help of her knees. Now her whole weight balanced on the strength of her fingers and a good positioning of her legs. She moved like an inch worm, up a few inches with her hands, up a few inches with her legs, and so on and so on. At first Michael cheered her on, but then he went silent—she could not see him, but she wondered if he had passed out. If so, she could use her wings . . . but not until she was sure.

When she made it up twenty feet, she paused on the first branch to rest and check on Michael. He lay on his side, facing away from her, and did not respond to his name. Tink looked the other way, but Peter and the rest of the Darlings had not found her yet.

Here goes nothing, Tink thought, and soared from the branch to the rock with the help of her wings.

Michael did not move when she alighted next to him, and when she turned him over, his eyes were closed. His skin was ashen, like a doll. She took him up in her arms, and through his wet coat, she felt his shivers. They had only minutes to save him.

Her wings, not used to carrying extra weight, strained against even this small burden. Still, though they dipped once or twice and sent her toes diving into the cold creek, they brought her and Michael to the other side unharmed. Tink didn't have time to carry him all the way home—even a few more minutes of hypothermia could kill him—so she flew up to the branch, gathered all of Michael's treehouse supplies, and carried the sticks back to the ground. The silver lighter was still in her pocket; this, along with her own coat, would serve as starter enough for a fire.

Flip. Position. Cock thumb. Light.

The glow was extraordinary. Tink stripped Michael of his wet coat, his flannel shirt, his jeans. Underneath he wore just his underwear, blue with smiling trains that under normal circumstances Tink would have described as creepy but now, in her panic, she found oddly comforting. She slipped his tiny body into her own shirt, her coat, her socks, and pressed him to her chest in order to add extra warmth to the heat of the fire. Inside her clothes, he was like a shrunken man. She wondered if he would die; she wondered if she should try to take him back to Neverland, even though the camp of Lost Boys had already reached a hundred. *He could take Peter's place,* she thought, and in that moment, she realized that if she didn't do something soon, Peter was never coming back with her.

"Tink?" Michael asked weakly.

"Oh thank goodness." Tink squeezed him tightly until he coughed. "Sorry. I just thought—"

"I fell," Michael said. "I just wanted to build a treehouse like Peter, but I couldn't hold up the sticks, and I—"

"Shh." She squeezed him again. "You don't need to explain yourself to me."

How many Lost Boys had she had this exact conversation with? How many of them had used those exact words—"like Peter"—and how many times had she wondered if they would make it until morning.

Speaking of Peter, he emerged soon after that with Wendy and John following close behind him. The three bent around Michael and Tink, all of them asking questions—Why did you run off? Were you trying to get yourself killed?—but Tink silenced them with one word: *Enough.*

"Michael's had a trying day," she continued. "I think it's best for him if we save our questions for tomorrow."

Michael burrowed further into her, his new protector. Peter huffed; Wendy smiled. John seemed relieved, probably because he would have felt personally responsible if Michael had been harmed on his watch. He took his brother up in his own coat and carried him all the way home, whispering brotherly things that no one else felt right overhearing.

"It's not my fault," Peter said to the girls during their walk. "He just ran off—"

"Silly Peter," Tink said, and the word *silly* suddenly meant something entirely new. Peter shrank away from the word. "If you want to grow into a man, you'd better start acting like one."

Before he could make any other excuses, Tink veered off the path and headed toward her cabin. The cold had begun to sink in—she wasn't wearing any clothes, after all—and all she wanted was to lie down in her own bed.

I'm not at all in love with Peter anymore, Tink realized as she lay there looking at the planks above her, much like the ones Peter had used to make his abandoned treehouse.

That night, she slept soundly for the first time in weeks.

CHAPTER TWENTY-FIVE

Godmother Anne's Introduction to "Mothers"

Excerpt from *Neverland: A History*

DID I CONSIDER MYSELF A KIND of mother to Tinker Bell?

Yes, I must admit that I did.

But not a very good one.

CHAPTER TWENTY-SIX

Now

TINK FLIES TO THE ONLY PLACE she can think of, the tree where so many years before young Michael tried to build his failed treehouse. Not much has changed about this part of the forest: same tall oak trees, bare and gangly without their leaves, like a crowd of young boys; same creek, wide and whispering with its stomach full of melted snow, like a snake stuffed with fallen Never bird eggs. Like Neverland, this place has stayed exactly the same, even as the retail district has expanded and encroached on most of the other land between the Darling mansion and town. This place is its own kind of tomb.

She floats to the branch of the tree Michael fell from—or at least what she thinks is the branch of the tree, considering there are now five that stretch across the creek. Like hands trying to meet in prayer, they are mirrored with the same number of branches from the trees on the other side.

As soon as her feet find secure grounding on the branch, she is suddenly transported to another time, a long-ago time, when her feet found the same balance on the yard of the Jolly Roger.

Seagulls crying in the distance.

Waves lapping at the hull.

No, Tink thinks, pulling herself back into the present by focusing on the cold. *It is winter. I am in New York.*

"Ahoy, Captain Hook!" Peter cries.

You're not real. This isn't real.

"Ahoy, you damned sprite." Captain Hook is far below them, just a tri-corner hat and some shiny black boots.

"Hey, I'm the sprite!" Tink volleys back.

No. That was then. This is now.

Tink focuses on the creek, and the way parts of it have frozen and are floating like little islands downstream. Islands that remind her of Neverland. Water that reminds her of the choppy waves near Hangman's Cove.

That was then. This is—

"If you're so brave," Hook says, brandishing his jeweled sword, "then why don't you come down and fight me like a man."

Tink looks at Peter, whose chest has puffed out like a bird protecting its nest. The sun shines in his eyes, two blazing fires of fury. His hair ruffles in the wind.

"Ready?" he asks.

"Ready," she says.

Together, they leap off of the yard, past the main topsail, and down the mast. Peter is like a hawk diving toward its prey; as he falls he lets out a cry that is something between a howl and a whoop. His body, sleek and shining with perspiration from his task, draws her eye again. While they drop, Tink realizes with a sudden shock that she is in love with Peter.

Peter puts out his hand.

Tink presses her fingers lightly into the palm of his hand, dusting the skin with fairy dust.

By the time they come to an abrupt stop just inches from the deck, Peter has drawn his own sword. The sailors scatter, startled by this strange bird man attacking from the sky, and only Captain Hook remains. He, too, is fearless, and later, Tink will learn that he was fighting for his life. It is easier for a man to risk everything when he has nothing left to lose.

Peter strikes at Captain Hook, and the Captain, a better swordsman, slaps the blow away. The boy and man circle each other, encouraged by the sailors, and then strike again. Their swords clank and clink, and Tink thinks of her stall in the market, the way her hammer felt in her hand.

Like Peter's touch.

Like power.

"You fight like a boy," says Captain Hook. He has Peter cornered, but then Peter kicks back his feet and pushes off the wall that leads up the quarter deck. Now Peter is on the outside, and Captain Hook is the one with nowhere to run.

Tink wonders whether she should stop him from killing the pirate. Sure, Captain Hook is after the mermaid's gold, but life in Neverland is considered more sacred than anywhere else in the universe. Perhaps there is a way they can resolve this. A truce? A treaty?

Peter swirls the tip of his sword so that it flicks Captain Hook's weapon out of his hand. The other, his hook, already brands him as Peter's victim.

"Peter," Tink says softly, not wanting to startle him into giving Captain Hook an inch, "perhaps we should consider a parlay—"

"Don't worry, Tink," Peter says. He uses his sword to urge Captain Hook around to his left—toward the plank. "I'm not going to be the one to kill him."

Now she hears the furious thrashing far below them, where the hull meets the water. Now she realizes why Peter insisted on attacking now, right now, at the very minute when every morning the crocodile circles the Jolly Roger three times hoping for a snack. The very moment that a month ago he de-handed Hook and tossed his body part overboard, the way he tossed the threat of death behind him as he flew away. Peter knew every move before he even left the Home Under the Ground that morning.

Tink should be unsettled, but instead, she feels only admiration. Peter doesn't care about truces, or treaties, or the question of whether it's fair to kill a pirate who only wanted some useless coins. He doesn't care about anything but keeping his word: *Come back again and I'll feed him the rest of you.* Peter moves by the orders of his heart, unburdened by guilt, filled only with purpose. He will send this pirate over the edge, into the mouth of the crocodile, and then he will wipe his hands of the matter of Captain Hook for good.

Flying is not the only way to be free.

Peter lifts the sword to strike. Captain Hook, unable to let a child best him, chooses the crocodile. He takes three backward steps down the plank, pauses at the edge, and closes his eyes. Is he thinking of the woman he loved, the one Tink heard is responsible for all of this trouble? Is he thinking of his ship, the piece of his heart that will live on even after the crocodile swallows him whole? Is he thinking of nothing at all?

Hook is there, against the backdrop of Neverland's perfect blue sky, and then he is gone.

* * *

"I SHOULD HAVE STOPPED YOU." TINK says this out loud, because she knows Peter is there, lurking somewhere in the trees.

"I wouldn't have listened." Peter pops his head out from behind the trunk of her tree and circles it by hopping from branch to branch.

"I should have tried."

Peter shrugs.

"There were a lot of things I should have stopped you from doing."

Peter shrugs again. God, she is sick of his boyish shrugs, his boyish grins, his boyish everything because he will never grow up. His ghost is like a layer of ice over her heart that will never melt. If only she could go back in time to that day on the Jolly Roger, to that moment when she looked at Peter and thought *love*, and slap that silly thought for that silly boy right out of her head. What was it that she loved, really? His bravado? His devil-may-care attitude? His skills with a sword, and an arrow, and a knife?

No.

There was more to it than that, even she must admit it.

What she loved, put simply and yet most complexly, was his Peter-ness. His unique way of doing everything, from building a treehouse to swimming in the lagoon. His way of pausing right before he shot an animal for dinner and grinning at her. He was like a wild animal who would eat out of only her hand.

Tink's mind wanders, as it sometimes does in her lowest moments, to what Peter would be doing right now if he were still alive. Would he still be on Earth? Would he have finally grown up, and gotten a job, and learned to be a father?

Would he have finally learned to dance?

Would he and Wendy be waltzing in the Darlings' living room, their hair graying, their skin growing soft and folded in places like a napkin, their laugh lines betraying how utterly, completely, amazingly happy they've been? Would John and Michael be there too? And little Andrew, now older and happier than Tink ever saw him, never having met a fairy named Tink who made him steal candy bars from the gas station near his house because she wanted him to have fun?

Think of the children you've hurt, Tink. List them. Wendy, Peter, Andrew, John, Michael—

How poor Andrew had cried, chocolate smeared around his mouth, empty wrappers on his closet floor. Tink had not understood him then—her heart had been as frozen as the creek—but she thinks she understands him now.

Some people, like Tink and Peter, are born with winter in their hearts; some people, like Wendy and Andrew, are born with spring.

No wonder Peter and I fell in love with the same person, Tink thinks. They had both felt the sunshine of Wendy's weather and thought, *Maybe I could be like that, too. Maybe I—*

But winter can never be spring.

Some people are good, and some are bad . . .

. . . and all people get what they deserve.

CHAPTER TWENTY-SEVEN

Then

TINK KNEW THAT SHE HAD TO redouble her efforts if she hoped to get Peter to return to Neverland, and yet, what was the use? Nothing that Peter did, short of murder, would separate the pair. Wendy apparently didn't care if the Lost Boy unraveled her sweaters, or left the stove burners on high, or let a family of squirrels into the attic, where they proceeded to tap dance across the squeaky floorboard all night.

She was in love with him.

Tink knew that if she set up another prank, it had to be epic. It had to be the kind of prank that you tell your children about fifty years later when you explain that someone isn't in your life because they did that absolutely unforgivable thing.

And yet Wendy was in love with him.

And Tink was in love with Wendy.

And if Tink did an epic, absolutely unforgiveable thing and Wendy found out . . .

But what choice did Tink have? She was in charge of taking care of Peter, and that meant returning him home.

If he stayed in the real world he would die—tomorrow, or fifty years in the future, no different really in their finiteness—and that was truly unforgiveable. In the process, he might manage to kill the whole Darling family, too.

In the meantime, preparations for the Winter Ball went on around her. One Saturday morning, a knock came at the cottage door, and Tink found Wendy on her welcome mat dressed in her best sweater and shiny ballet flats. Her hair was pinned back behind her ears with bobby pins. Though she wasn't wearing makeup, her pale cheeks had a late fall glow from the chill.

"Hey," Tink said. She turned back toward the interior, where she had a pan of eggs on the stove, but left the door open behind her.

"Look at this place." Wendy walked in and closed the door. "It's even better than when Dad built it."

Tink didn't reply. Her eggs had gone from under to overcooked in the time it had taken her to let Wendy in, but she slid the chunks of dry egg onto her chipped blue plate and attacked them with a fork anyway in order to give herself something to do. She did not offer Wendy any.

"Anyway," Wendy said, "I came by because I wanted to ask if you'd . . . if maybe you might . . . Would you go shopping with me for a dress for the Ball?"

Tink raised one eyebrow and continued to skewer egg pieces.

"I know, I know, shopping is probably not your cup of tea, but I just thought . . . " Wendy tried to tuck her hair behind her ears, but it was already held there with a pin.

"We haven't gotten to spend a lot of time together since Michael's accident."

That's intentional, Tink thought. *Besides, how can I spend any time with you with Peter guarding you all the time?* She thought of the time when Peter had found a ruby in the cove off of Mermaids' Lagoon, and how he had immediately hidden it in a tree stump in order to keep his prize out of greedy Lost Boy hands. Every day he had visited the ruby, and when Tink followed him, she found him petting it like a child pets a kitten and whispering to it in a soft singsong. Finally, in order to get him to stop obsessing over his find, Tink had spent a night marking every stump in the forest with the same pattern of stripped bark. *Try to find your ruby now,* she had thought, and sure enough, Peter had cried and then forgotten all about it.

"Tink?"

Tink shook herself out of her memories. "What?"

"Will you go?"

The closer you are to Wendy, the better to form a plan to break them up.

"Sure," Tink said. She pushed her plate away. "But don't think for a second that you're getting me in one of those poufy gowns."

The mall was a chaotic display, a carnival of cheery salespeople and eager shoppers and colors colors colors. Tink had never been in a mall before, and the first thing she noticed after the displays was the sound, white noise of steps and music playlists and many conversations. Last came the smell, like there was a hidden field of flowers in the basement emitting their aromas—only their aromas had been corrupted by the food court and the chemicals used to clean the floor and the general sweat of bodies racing from store to store.

"This must be overwhelming," said Wendy over the din.

"Just a little."

A young woman in black leggings and an oversized black shirt approached Tink with her hand outstretched. "If I can just have ten seconds of your time . . . " she said. Too late, Tink noticed some kind of white stuff in her palm, which became warm and wet.

"Oh. No. Thanks. I'm not—"

"This is called our Refining Cream," the woman said. She looked like a model, but the kind you might see in a local commercial. Somehow, she was managing to both massage Tink's hand and pull her toward the kiosk. "If you'll just step over here, I'll show you the list of ingredients."

"No. Sorry. I don't want—"

"Feel how smooth your hands are?" The woman asked. Tink had to admit that her hands were soft. "That moisture comes from Aloe Vera. We also have a sea salt scrub—"

"She said no," Wendy said, and wrenched Tink's hand from the saleswoman.

Tink normally had no problem telling people to go away, but for some reason, this mall place seemed to paralyze her. There were too many people, too many noises, too many bright lights. Her head ached. She felt like that sweet-sweat smell was trying to suffocate her.

"Why don't we go in a department store?" Wendy

suggested, and Tink followed her gratefully onto new terrain. When they reached the formal dress section, Tink was overwhelmed by long sheaths of silk, chiffon, and tulle. Sequins on stiff bodices sparkled; rhinestones on belts gleamed. The colors were even brighter here: petal pink, eggplant purple, royal blue. Tink couldn't imagine Wendy wearing any of them.

"These are so . . . ," Tink held up a hanger on which hung a slinky white gown with cutouts in the sides, " . . . strange."

"I know." Wendy took the dress and put it back. "Why would I pay more for only part of a dress?"

"Why would you pay for a dress at all?"

"What do you mean?" Wendy asked. She was browsing through a row of emerald green gowns.

"I mean they're uncomfortable. You can't run, or jump, or—," Tink was going to say fly, "—other stuff."

"You're not supposed to do any of those things at a dance." Wendy disappeared behind a circular display of puffy pink dresses that looked like cupcakes with sparkly crowns on top, but her voice carried. "You're just supposed to dance."

"I know," said Tink, "but still. I'm not a doll—I don't want to be dressed up."

Tink ran her hand down a line of flared skirts and cringed. They reminded her of her uniform, and the way Godmother Anne had always reminded her girls of the three Fs: "feminine, flirty, flitting." The other fairies in the guard seemed happy with their assigned roles, and they had flirted and flitted and flown their iridescent selves to all corners of the universe. There wasn't a mirror pool in the middle of every fairy kingdom market for nothing.

"You act like someone's trying to force you into a dress," said Wendy. "If you don't like them, don't wear them."

"I won't," said Tink grumpily. She was thinking of Peter, and the way he would look at Wendy when he saw her in one of those gowns. Easy for a girl like Wendy to say not to bother.

Wendy carried a few dresses into the dressing rooms, and Tink sat on a short bench in the dressing room opposite her with the door open. There was a lot of rustling, and then Wendy emerged in what Tink could only describe as a carnivorous tulle flower trying to swallow Wendy whole.

"Ugh," Tink exclaimed. Then she put her hands over her mouth. "Sorry, did you . . . ?"

"God no," said Wendy. "I look like a cake topper."

"I'm glad you said it first," said Tink.

Back into the dressing room Wendy went. The next two dresses were equally hideous, one a strapless corset with a slit so high Tink averted her eyes and the other something called a "mermaid" dress, though Tink could testify that the green, sequined monstrosity in front of her looked nothing like a real mermaid's fleshy tail.

"How would a mermaid swim with all of that glittery goop?" Tink asked. "And besides, mermaids aren't—," she was going to say green, "—real."

"Of course not," said Wendy. She examined herself in the mirror and wrinkled her nose. "Plus, how am I supposed to dance if I can't move my knees?"

When Wendy came out in the last dress, Tink let out a whistle. Unlike the other gowns, this one was much more practical: it had straps, no boning, and a full-bodied skirt good for running, or jumping, or even flying—though descending would be a big reveal. Even the color, a midnight blue, would help with camouflage.

"What do you think?" asked Wendy. She spun around, and the skirt lifted and then resettled.

"It's . . . practical."

"Oh great."

"No, I mean, it's practical in a good way. You don't look like a doll or something, you look . . . " *Beautiful. Breathtaking. I love you, Wendy, since the moment I—* " . . . pretty."

"Really?"

Tink nodded. She suddenly wished she had not agreed to come. There was a flirty, flitting fairy in her chest, and though it wasn't feminine, it desired the person in front of her who was. Tink tried to force the fairy back into the cage of her heart, but it beat against the walls there too.

"I should get back," Tink said. She stood up, suddenly aware of her dirty boots, her unwashed hair, the holes in her sweatshirt where her nervous fingers had slowly worn through the cuffs of her sleeves. She was suddenly aware that to Wendy, she was nothing but wallpaper. Whatever moment they had shared that night when she gave Wendy the leaf, it had passed. She needed to get out of that dressing room, out of that mall, out of that town and planet and universe.

"Wait, Tink." Wendy grabbed her arm.

"What?" Tink asked. Her voice was so harsh that even she recoiled.

"I never got a chance to say I'm sorry for what happened. That night when you . . . and then Peter . . . I could have handled that so much better." She let go of Tink but held her gaze. "I really do like you both. I just got carried away in the moment, and then things just sort of . . . happened between Peter and me. And now, no matter how I feel about you, I need to honor that thing that happened."

"This isn't the eighteenth century," said Tink. "You're not bound to him just because you hooked up in the forest." She hadn't meant to reveal what she'd seen, and she didn't want to fight with Wendy, especially when she knew that both she and Peter needed to leave, yet there she was, fighting.

"It's not that." Wendy's face turned bright red.

"Then what?" Tink said too loud. She had lost control again, and the fairy in her chest was a furious pounding.

"I'm pregnant," Wendy whispered.

Instantly, the pounding stopped.

CHAPTER TWENTY-EIGHT

"The Pirate War"

Excerpt from *Neverland: A History*

THOUGH EVERYONE HAS HEARD OF THE Pirate War and its effects on the entire magical realm, not many people know the story of how the conflict actually began. Peter Pan's part in Captain Hook's demise was only the last move in a long chess game dating back to before Neverland existed, and it started not with a boy, or a crocodile, but a kiss.

Before we begin, a word about the structure of pirate bureaucracy: although every ship has a Captain, and that Captain is a free agent aiming his ship's wheel in whichever direction the wind whispers, there is one person—the Pirate King—to whom he must answer, and of course pay taxes. Not regularly, not even yearly, but centennially, at the Seventeen Seas Gala.

It just so happened that the year of the Sixteenth Gala, one Captain James Hook had just taken the helm of the Jolly Roger after a bloody mutiny and was attending the event for the first time. In the weeks leading up to the event, other pirates he met at the ports warned him about Marianna Blackbeard, daughter and first mate to her father, Captain Blackbeard—*Whatever happens,* they said, *you mustn't fall in love with her*—but Captain Hook was nonplussed. He only had room in his heart for one lady, and that was the Jolly Roger, mate of his soul.

Or so he thought until he lay eyes on Marianna.

Her skin was the color of sand. Her eyes were as blue as the ocean. Her hair was a wave of curly brown tresses. Her greenish-blue gown had a white layer of foamy tulle that only showed when she took a step.

Can you really blame a pirate for falling in love with such a watery woman?

When Captain Hook asked the fine lady for a dance, the jealous Captain Blackbeard took notice. When he stole her away to the back gardens, the jealous Captain Blackbeard sent two of his finest sailors to watch over her. And when Captain Hook floated a kiss onto Marianna's sandy cheek, the jealous Captain Blackbeard ordered his men to pillage until not a single gold coin remained on the Jolly Roger.

Needless to say, the Pirate King was not pleased when Captain Hook had nothing to submit as payment the next morning.

You have one hundred years, he pronounced from his gold throne, which was made of fused coins and jewels so dazzling that they blinded anyone brought in front of him, *to produce one hundred times your taxes. If, after that time, you cannot produce the proper amount, you will be stripped of your title and your ship burned.*

Captain Hook agreed to the terms—what choice did he have?—but he knew that a treasure like the one the Pirate King required would be impossible to find. Still, he had to try, so he and his men scoured the realms looking for old maps that might lead to even older treasures. As mentioned in the introduction to this volume, one such treasure lay at the bottom of Mermaids' Lagoon.

What is most interesting to me as a historian is that the events of the past have a way of repeating themselves, echoing like waves returning again and again to the shore.

Captain Hook fell in love with the wrong woman, and therefore, he came to Neverland in search of a treasure to redeem himself in the Pirate King's eyes. And because Captain Hook came to Neverland, Peter Pan and Tinker Bell had to work together to fight him off.

And because they had to work together to fight him off, Tinker Bell fell in love with the wrong man.

CHAPTER TWENTY-NINE

Now

When Tink lands in the front yard of the Darling house, Hope is sitting on the front steps waiting for her. The cold and wind have stung her round cheeks a sharp red, and she is missing one of her gloves. Her hair, so straight before, is whipped into a nest. Tink hasn't seen her smile so big since she arrived.

"That was incredible," Hope says as if she just touched down, even though she must have been sitting there for at least half an hour waiting for Tink. "I can't believe you can fly whenever you want to."

"Well, I don't want to," says Tink. She wants to be alone, and Hope has become a nuisance. "I'm going home."

Tink turns toward the cottage and manages a few steps before she hears Hope following her.

"Why don't you like flying?"

Tink stops and lets out a very long sigh. "Because flying reminds me of Peter, okay?"

"But it's so wonderf—"

"I'm going home," Tink says again, but Hope doesn't seem to want to let her be alone. Their steps become a kind of rhythm, crunching hard into the snow.

"You know," says Hope quietly, "I used to play basketball. Like, for my high school. I got scholarship offers and everything. But when dad died, I just . . . stopped."

Tink soldiers ahead. She is not in the mood for group therapy.

"Last month, I was walking home from class, and I saw these kids playing a pickup game in the park. I can't explain why, but for some reason, I asked to join them. And you know what?"

"What?" asks Tink, despite her determination not to engage.

"I had a great time."

Tink rolls her eyes. "Great. So you're telling me I should just start flying again because I'll have a great time?"

"Let me finish." Hope stops walking, and Tink can't help stopping too. "I had a great time, and then I felt so guilty that I went back to the court that night and spray-painted graffiti all over it. Like, really bad stuff I can't repeat. They had to completely pave over the blacktop, which took almost a month, and by then, it was too hot to play outside."

Tink has to admit she's impressed. Spray painting a public park to ease her own twisted guilt is exactly the kind of thing she would do.

"Come on," Tink says, and starts to walk again. "I'll make you a cup of coffee to warm you up.

* * *

WHEN THEY GET BACK TO HER cottage, Tink puts a pot of coffee on and then opens the room's only closet. Several objects fall off the pile: a dirty baseball, a cowboy hat, a spaghetti strainer. "I know it's here somewhere," she says, and leans on the pile in order to look through a row of hanging clothes protected by plastic bags.

"What?" asks Hope. She is sitting at the table watching the search.

"This." Tink pulls one of the bags out and then tries to shut the door, meeting with resistance from a fur coat that had been Wendy's great-grandmother's. "Wendy's dress."

"Is that really it?" Hope leaps up and takes the bag out of Tink's hands. She rips through the gray plastic bag to the interior, where a midnight blue satin gown hangs from a cheap plastic hanger. "It's just like you described. Only . . . " She holds up the tag. "She never wore it."

"No she didn't." Tink places her hand lightly on the dress and imagines Wendy wearing it. "But I need more coffee before I can tell that story."

"In the meantime, mind if I . . . ?"

"Try it on?" Tink does mind, but she knows she shouldn't. Besides, the dress and everything else on the Darling property belongs to Hope. "Go ahead."

While Tink pours their drinks, Hope goes in the bathroom to change. Tink's hands are shaking, and when she takes a few sips of coffee, their quaking escalates. From the cabinet below, she pulls out a bottle of Irish whiskey and pours a generous amount into her cup, then gulps down the rest of the coffee in three long swigs. The pairing, hot and stinging, burns her throat as it goes down. Still, she feels instantly calmer. Then she refills her flask with whiskey.

"Well?" Hope is standing in the bathroom doorway. Tink wonders if she saw the bottle. "What do you think?"

"You look . . . " Tink evaluates the dress, too small for Hope's tall frame, too dark for her pale skin. She looks like a shirt that's been washed too many times, stretched to the point of breaking. " . . . terrible."

"I know, right?" Hope twirls. The dress is not even zipped in the back. "My grandmother was apparently at least three sizes smaller than me and a completely different skin tone."

"Yes, she was." Tink returns to the closet and digs a little more. This time, she retrieves a zippered dress bag, black but dusty to the point of grayness. "Try this one instead."

Hope gives her a questioning look but doesn't argue. Tink returns to the counter, gulps down another drink—this time minus the coffee—and waits. When Hope opens the door this time, she is a vision in a wool skirt suit cut to her exact curves and fur neck wrap.

"Much better," says Tink.

"These belonged to Wendy too?" Hope spins again, this time with all of her clothes securely attached. The knee-length skirt pats her knees.

"Of course not. You think Wendy wore a suit from the 1930s?" Tink walks over and touches the thick wool. "This suit belonged to Peter's mother."

"Peter's mother?" Hope seems confused. "But didn't she—"

"Abandon him?" Tink straightens Hope's collar. "For a long time Peter dreamed of reuniting with her . . . until the day he actually did. She had moved on, had another child, and forgotten him. Peter was heartbroken, and he never went back. I stole this for him just in case he ever wanted something of hers, but he did what every Lost Boy does in Neverland: forgot all about her." Tink still remembers the look on Peter's face when he turned away from the window.

"He forgot his own mother?" Hope asks.

"Everyone forgets everything, in time." This is not quite true—Tink remembers everything—but she is not sure she wants to admit that yet. There are still parts of Peter and Wendy's story she wants to keep to herself.

"I don't know if that's—"

A knock interrupts whatever Hope was about to say.

"Expecting company?" Hope asks.

"Never."

Tink goes to the door and looks through the peephole. Amidst the late afternoon sunlight reflected on the snow, a woman with purple hair and movie star sunglasses stands too close to the glass.

"Uh . . . Hope?" Tink asks.

"Yes?"

Tink turns around. "I think your mom is at my door."

CHAPTER THIRTY

Then

TINK AND WENDY DROVE TO THE pharmacy in silence. Wendy, normally a careful driver no matter the destination, was even more careful that day, seeming completely absorbed in adjusting her rearview mirror or signaling for a turn. Tink wished she had something to do with her own hands, which sat in her lap like two dead fish, so she decided to scroll through the radio stations. *Pop-rock-Christian-pop-country.* Tink didn't know any of the songs; the last time Tink had listened to music in a car had been in the winter of 1964, after the Beatles released "I Want to Hold Your Hand" and the song hit number one in America. Technically, she hadn't been "in" a vehicle but on top of one, riding a truck like a wild bronco with Peter behind her hanging from the door handle, a boy-shaped flag flapping in the wind. Still, whatever booming beat was coming out of the Honda's front speakers was no "I Want to Hold Your Hand."

"Isn't that . . . ?" Tink asked as they drove past the pharmacy.

Wendy had to make a U-turn at the next light. As she coasted into the parking lot, she let out a long, slow breath through her teeth, and Tink realized it was probably taking everything inside of her not to lose her cool. *How hard,* Tink thought, *to always have to be responsible. How grown-up.*

The pharmacy reminded Tink of an industrial garden, set in rows and sectioned off by type of product. They even had a stack of baskets, from which Wendy pulled the top bin. After a short search Wendy found the sign that said Family Planning, and Tink tried not to laugh at the irony. The tests were in pink, purple, and blue boxes, and Wendy quickly grabbed a purple one and put it in her basket. Her cheeks turned pink. On the way to the checkout station, she covered the box with a bag of pretzels, three individual toilet paper rolls, and a loofa. Tink had wanted to try something called "sour straws," but she decided now was not the time to make grocery requests.

Tink expected a nosy cashier, but instead, the woman behind the counter typed on the keys in front of her and then wordlessly accepted a twenty-dollar bill. Tink wondered if Wendy had chosen this particular pharmacy because she thought it would be safer, and decided yes, because Wendy never did anything carelessly. Even the way she put her items into the bag—pretzels first, test on top, toilet paper rolls on either side, and the luffa on top—was planned ahead of time.

Once the test was secured, Wendy walked across the parking lot to a McDonalds and Tink followed her.

Again, Wendy made a show of purchasing something—a double cheeseburger—in order to use the restroom without drawing suspicion. On her way to the bathroom, she chucked the uneaten burger into the trash can, and then disappeared into the single-person stall.

Tink didn't know what to do, so she sat down at the table closest to the bathroom, wishing she had that burger to occupy her hands. Not that she could have eaten anything—her stomach was in knots—but she could have nibbled or just ripped the burger bun to pieces. As it was, she could only zip and unzip her hoodie.

There was a thick pane of glass next to her, and through it, she turned and watched children playing on an activity gym while their mothers and fathers congregated at a single table on the far side of the room. They all seemed to be having a good time. The children were screaming loud enough for the sound to come through the glass, while the parents smiled big and talked quietly among themselves. None of the children wore shoes, and Tink wondered how many feet had stepped in those same plastic tunnels. She thought of the Lost Boys, fatherless now as well as motherless, and wondered if they remembered her.

It took Tink a minute to notice Wendy standing next to her.

She stood up.

"Are you . . . ?"

Wendy didn't say a word, hadn't said a word since the dressing room, and yet when she put out her hand, Tink knew to take it and squeeze.

* * *

WENDY TOLD PETER THAT NIGHT. TINK wasn't there—no one else was—but she watched them from her perch in a tree near Wendy's window. She was glad they had chosen that room for their midnight rendezvous, since Peter knew better and always kept his curtains drawn. "Peter," Tink imagined Wendy saying as she took his hand. "We're going to have a baby."

When Peter stood up and bolted, Tink wasn't surprised. It was why she was waiting in the branches of an oak tree. A minute passed, and then the boy-becoming-a-man ran from the Darling house, across the yard, and right toward the place where Tink waited, his long legs carrying him almost as fast as flying would.

"Tink," he yelled, as if he could sense her. His breath came up to her in little fogs. He had not stopped to put on a coat, and now his skinny, bare arms shook.

"Yes, Peter?"

"I want to go back to Neverland."

The moment had finally come. Tink took inventory of her feelings and discovered she felt no joy in the pronouncement, just the dull ache of sadness.

"Very well," she said, shaking her wings a little so that a sprinkle of fairy dust fell like snow on Peter's head. "Let's go home."

The night was fair for flying. The clouds seemed to blanket them; the breezes seemed to urge them on. Earth was a ball shot into the distance, growing smaller and smaller until Neverland took its place. Tink had not flown this way in months, and yet she did not spin or cartwheel or dart. In fact, she was hunched, as was Peter beside her—like two pallbearers with a heavy load.

"Straight on till morning?" Tink asked, their catch-phrase coming out as a question.

Peter didn't say anything.

PART THREE

CHAPTER THIRTY-ONE

"Peter and Tinker Bell"

Excerpt from *Neverland: A History*

By this point, readers are likely wondering what Peter Pan thought about Tinker Bell's affection. Did he know how she felt about him? Did he ever return the sentiment?

Though we can never know for certain, especially since the Lost Boys have long since forgotten poor Peter, interviews with Tinker Bell, the Darlings, and the inhabitants of Neverland indicate that he may have been more aware of her adoration than he let on. One event in particular stands out, and I will relay it here for your judgment.

After the Pirate War ended with a crocodile's snack, things in the Home Under the Ground returned to business as usual. However, the terrain of Tinker Bell's heart had shifted significantly. She tried to act the same around Peter Pan, participating in the same pranks and general mischief of the Lost Boys, but apparently even the disinterested mermaids noticed a change in her behavior. She blushed. She laughed too indiscriminately at Peter's jokes. She stalked him on his visits to the Kandallanians and especially to the chief's daughter, Tiger Lily. For a fairy who prided herself on her devil-may-care attitude, she seemed to care a great deal.

One afternoon—as happens in Neverland, no one knows when, but it might have been about forty years ago—Peter Pan and Tinker Bell were returning from a swim in Mermaids' Lagoon when a single Never tree leaf, rustled free from its stem by a squirrel, fell into Tinker Bell's upturned palm. The red, heart-shaped leaf startled Tink, who had been making a point about the Kandallanians—they were then in the habit of taking all of the ripe Never fruit and drying it for storage, therefore hogging all of the bounty—by gesticulating wildly with the hand turned up in the air.

"Oh," she'd said, and looked at Peter. "Do you want—"

"Look, that one is covered in Never tree sap!" Peter had exclaimed. Then he'd plucked the leaf from her hand, pressed it face-down on his tongue, and swallowed it whole.

Now, before we judge Peter too harshly, we must consider that he likely hadn't recalled the tradition of the Never tree leaf when he claimed the sappy red heart and ate it. He likely considered his good buddy Tink so far removed from the possibility of romance that she couldn't have given him the leaf as anything but a prank, and had consumed it without a second thought.

Or, maybe, we must judge him all the more harshly for these actions.

After all, Peter was always cruelest when he least intended it.

CHAPTER THIRTY-TWO

Then

NEVERLAND WAS THE REAL WORLD, AND the real world was a dream. Tink woke from it in her bed, in her apartment, in the Home Under the Ground, and she had to work through her position this way, to situate herself by the acorn crown hanging on the wall and the gossamer webs of spiders who every night wove their tapestries over the portholes. If she closed her eyes, she could almost feel Wendy's hand on her arm, but the feeling dissipated and was replaced with the excitement of a new day in Neverland.

Tink rose and looked through the cloudy panes of glass, from which she could watch the Lost Boys milling about their courtyard. Tink's apartment was slightly lower than the center square, which meant she saw mostly feet and knees stomping back and forth across the packed dirt. Above her were underground trees that survived on the bit of light filtered down the hole in the high ceiling of the room, and in those trees, each Lost Boy had his very own treehouse.

There was no coffee in Neverland—coffee was unarguably a grown-up drink—but there was hot cocoa, which

Tink fixed with cream and ten marshmallows that melted into the chocolate like ships sinking into the sea. She carried her thermos out the door, a slab of wood that showed the rings of its Never tree parent and had to be rolled away every time she came or went, and stepped up into the square.

"Morning, Tink," said Little Ben, tipping his pointed hat.

"Morning, Little Ben," said Tink.

Little Ben flipped his hat three times in the air, caught it, and righted it on his head.

"Off to Mermaids' Lagoon?" asked Little Samuel, who carried a hatchet in one hand and a kite in the other.

"Not today," said Tink.

Everywhere, Lost Boys were swinging or sliding down from their trees, depending on whether they'd chosen a rope or a slide for their playing pleasure. Though all treehouses were fashioned from the wood of Never trees and straw from the grasses around the lagoon, they were decorated to different degrees depending on how long a Lost Boy had lived there. Little Samuel's house, for example, was painted berry blue, the result of many hours of squishing berries between his toes like an Italian winemaker might squish grapes, while Little Ben had only threaded a few flowers into the thatched roof.

Peter Pan's house was all the way on the other side of the courtyard, in the tallest, widest tree. His house was not only painted green from leaf pigment, but had strings of berry garlands adorning its façade. His mode of entry was a stately ladder, which the Lost Boys rarely climbed. The chimes on Peter's door had been a gift from Tink, and were made of mermaid glass she'd traded for fairy dust. Oh, how silly the mermaids had looked flying around Neverland that day, flopping their tails back and forth like swinging sails, but the look on Peter's face when he'd heard the tinkling had been worth it.

Tink climbed up the rungs and knocked on Peter's door.

"Come in," said a dreary voice.

Peter's house was dark. All of the curtains, hides from animals caught and skinned by Tiger Lily's clan, were drawn. His covers were pulled up to his forehead, though she could hear him breathing deeply against the fabric. The room smelled like clothes left in the hamper for too long and old chicken noodle soup, which Tink had brought the day before and still sat on the table, a film of fat floating on top.

"Peter?" Tink sat down on the bed and pulled back the sheet.

Peter Pan's eyes stayed looking up at the wall. His legs and arms were straight and stiff, like a man already dead. Slowly, his head turned toward her.

"Hello, Tink," he said in a dull voice.

"Good morning, Peter." Tink's voice was ten times more cheerful than normal. "I thought maybe you could get out of bed today, visit the cove? Or we could fly to the forest and catch—"

"I don't think I'm up for an adventure today," Peter said. "I'm afraid I'm not myself."

Tink had heard it all before—163 times, in fact. Every morning since she and Peter had returned from the real world, they played through their lines, always ending in the same defeated silence and Tink's withdrawal. Still, she tried to lure him out.

"That's okay. You just need to fly a little while, and you'll feel like a whole new Peter."

"Sorry Tink. I wish I knew why I feel this way, but I don't. Maybe tomorrow?" Up went the covers. Tink knew that no matter what she said, Peter would not emerge again until the following morning.

She left him and went back into the courtyard. The Lost Boys had not completely forgotten Peter when he and Tink returned, but they hadn't exactly remembered him, either; Tink had worked hard to spread the lore of Peter's founding as the original Lost Boy, and to tell the stories of the many adventures they'd had together over the fire as the Lost Boys ate toasted marshmallows and chocolate bars. Now, again, he was disappearing from memory. Every once in a while, one of the Lost Boys would ask, *Hey, where's Peter?* but more and more, they were finding ways to survive without their fearless leader.

Tink couldn't blame them.

Their fearless leader was gone.

"How's Peter?" Little Ben asked from behind her. He had always been Peter's most devoted fan, and since Peter's disappearance he had taken to dressing in a knockoff version of Peter's red tunic and green hat.

"Better," Tink lied. She had seen enough sadness for one day. "He just needs time."

"What happened to him out there?" Little Ben asked. He had asked her this many times before, but he had forgotten them all.

"He grew up a little," Tink said.

"I don't ever want to grow up," Little Ben said solemnly.

Tink patted his hat fondly. "Don't worry, Little Ben. You won't."

The day passed slowly. Without Peter's mischief, the Lost Boys had settled into a kind of routine: food fight in the early morning, chores after that, a second food fight after lunch, naps, and then a bonfire until the stars came out. Fun, fun, fun, but they lacked Peter's imagination. Back in his reign, they had stolen eggs from the Never bird, made sauce from Never fruit by holding a smashing contest, and built a slide so long it took boys from the top of the highest hill all the way into Mermaids' Lagoon. Not that they knew the difference, since they forgot everything almost the minute it happened, but Tink knew. She had watched their games from the sidelines and reveled in their joy.

To distract herself, Tink decided to fly to Mermaids' Lagoon. The boys whooped at her as she shot through the tunnel and out the hole, and then she was through the branches of the Never trees and above the forest. How small her problems looked from that view. Seagulls flapped beneath her and fell behind, their white wings practically in slow motion compared to the flit of her own. The day was a perfect eighty degrees, sunny but clouded so that she never had to shield her eyes. Neverland was a map beneath her.

Mermaid's Lagoon appeared as a darker blue swatch with a circle of tan beaches and, beyond both, the bright blue sea. Tink adjusted her flight and sailed down to the shore. She was careful to check for sunning mermaids, but they seemed to be enjoying the water that day.

Almost as soon as she touched down, her dainty fairy shoes filled with sand.

"Ugh," said Tink, who hated the feeling of dry sand on her skin.

"Hello to you, too," said a voice from behind a rock.

Tink tiptoed cautiously around the obstruction. Mermaids were always vain but occasionally vicious, and they had been known to try to drown a Lost Boy or sailor when the mood struck them. This one, luckily, was Andalain, and she was the reason that Tink had come to Mermaids' Lagoon in the first place. Tink knew her from her hair, which was a seashell pink, and from the fact that she was taller and broader shouldered than any other mermaid. Even before their trip to the real world, Tink had used Andalain as her confidant. As magical creatures themselves, the mermaids did not have the forgetfulness of the boys, who were, after all, only human.

"You mermaids really have a way of blending in," said Tink as she hovered just enough to perch on the rock. Andalain's tail was the color of the sand, and the shiny scales reflected the texture of their surroundings. Her top half was also that color, though the skin there was smooth and almost tough, like a dolphin. Tink knew this because she and Andalain had once gotten drunk on wine Tink had made from Never fruit, and Andalain had let her touch the place below her collar bone for a few seconds before telling her that if Tink ever told the other mermaids, Andalain would send her to the bottom of the ocean.

"I can't say the same for you," Andalain said slowly. Like most mermaids, she talked like she was half asleep, though Tink suspected it was vanity that made them confident their listeners would stick around.

"Yeah, well, the Godmothers seem really stuck on these shiny skirts."

Tink sat down on the rock and crossed her legs. Andalain rolled over so that her back could get some sun, but she gave Tink the courtesy of looking in her direction.

"Peter's still in bed," said Tink.

"Oh really?" asked Andalain. "He hasn't . . . " she paused for a full minute, " . . . gotten over losing the love of his life yet? How . . . " she blinked for a full ten seconds, " . . . inconvenient of him."

Tink started to roll her eyes but thought better of it. People had been drowned for less.

"What should I do?" Tink asked.

"Well . . . " Andalain pulled her long hair up and twisted it, revealing a slender neck and the two dunes of her shoulders. " . . . We mermaids have a saying . . . " She closed her eyes and snuggled into the sand.

"What's the saying?"

"Oh, right . . . " Andalain opened her eyes again. "'A fish without water is just dinner.'"

" . . . *That's* your advice to me?" Tink stood up on the rock and began pacing the short distance between edges. "Peter's depressed and the Lost Boys are forgetting him and Wendy is pregnant and I'm miserable and you're *telling me about fish*?" Her voice was an uncomfortable volume. From the lagoon, a few curious mermaid heads emerged, and one of them bared her teeth.

"Sorry, sorry." Tink forced herself to take a deep breath and then sat back down.

"I only meant . . . " Andalain rolled back over again, unbothered, " . . . that without Wendy, Peter can't be himself . . . So it seems to me . . . if you want Peter Pan back . . . you must . . . "

" . . . Must what?"

"Reunite them." Andalain waved her hand slightly in a flourish and then flopped it back on the sand.

Tink sighed. "A lot of help you are, Andalain. We've been over this: if I reunite them, then Peter will die."

"You know, we mermaids have a saying . . . A fish out of water—"

"—is just dinner. Yeah, I get it. Peter will just lie here wasting his immortality, so I might as well reunite them, right? Is that what you're saying?"

Andalain shrugged. "I don't care one way or the other. 'A single fish in the ocean—'"

Tink didn't have the patience to listen to any more mermaid talk, so she pushed off the rock and caught herself on an updraft. Andalain had been no help, so on the way back to the Home Under the Ground, she thought about her other options. Tink knew that she should go to the fairy kingdom and ask Godmother Anne what to do, but she was afraid of what her leader would propose. Wiping Peter clean, perhaps, or removing him from Neverland altogether? Tink had been responsible for enough destruction in the name of Peter's immortality; she couldn't bear it if, after all that had happened, that was taken from him too.

But what was an immortal life without a moment of happiness?

No life at all.

A fish without water—

Curse that sandy mermaid and her platitudes.

Tink flew back down the hole and alighted on one of the slides.

"Coming to the bonfire, Tink?" Little Stephen asked as he passed by. He had a bundle of logs under his right arm just the right size and shape for burning.

"I don't think so, Little Stephen," she said.

"Makes sense." Little Stephen looked up at the tree branches visible through the hole above them. "It's flying weather."

"What did you say?" Tink asked, but Little Stephen had disappeared into a sea of Lost Boys getting ready for the fire.

It's flying weather.

A fish without water is just dinner.

Peter can't be himself without Wendy.

Oh no, Tink thought, and then she stood up so fast the whole courtyard spun. *What have I done?*

CHAPTER THIRTY-THREE

"Mermaids"

Excerpt from *Neverland: A History*

ALTHOUGH NEVERLAND WAS A KIND OF utopia, all of the groups who inhabited the island were actually quite violent. The Kandallanians had ritually sacrificed the lower caste on Kandallan—a group called the Mandallanians—before the Mandallanians rose up and took control of the planet; the Lost Boys had a tendency of letting their pranks become dangerous or even life-threatening; and the mermaids, well . . . they were a different thing entirely.

What made them so frightening was that no one understood why they did the things they did. The Kandallanians had an organized religion around sacrifice, the Lost Boys were consumed by their desires for fun, but the mermaids drowned creatures at random for no purpose whatsoever. Not all the time, of course—we wouldn't have allowed such coldblooded killers into Neverland—but only occasionally, when the mood struck them. One minute a naughty Lost Boy was playing with the tail of a sleeping mermaid, and the next, that Lost Boy had to be fished out of Mermaids' Lagoon.

As I said, a different thing entirely.

Some Tag researchers believed that the mermaids' violence stemmed from their upbringing. Though the beautiful creatures were almost godly in Neverland, on their home planet, they were nothing more than a delicacy for the giants who enjoyed a good fried mermaid tail—sans scales. Their deaths were made more gruesome by the fact that the mermaids would be kept alive until the final sauté; their scales were removed while they were fully awake and screaming.

Imagine it. One minute a mermaid would be swimming through the ocean, long hair flowing like seaweed in a current; the next, she would find herself hauled up in a net and dumped into a pool filled to the lip with sullied seawater and half-dead sisters.

Much like the Lost Boys and Kandallanians they attacked, wouldn't you say?

And yet, there were other theories about their violence, theories that went back to before the giants, before man, before anything or anyone but the ocean and its prehistoric creatures. Brain chemistry, survival instincts, a slew of other explanations. All plausible, and yet none, in my opinion, correct.

So what did I believe caused the mermaids to attempt murder?

Us.

The forgetfulness spell we put on the island was only supposed to affect humans, who had weaker brains and a strong motivation for wanting to forget their sad pasts. But what if some of that forgetfulness washed away the mermaids' memory of consequences? What if we had whited out the control mechanisms of their brains?

Would that make us murderers too?

CHAPTER THIRTY-FOUR

Now

"DON'T LET HER IN," HOPE INSTRUCTS. Her mother is knocking again, the kind of light but persistent tapping that indicates the person on the other side already knows you're home. Her movie star sunglasses make her look like a bug from Tink's warped peephole view.

"We can't just ignore her," says Tink. The knocking has already moved from her ears to her brain and is tat-tat-tatting away in her vulnerable head. "She obviously knows we're here."

"She can't." Hope is unbuttoning the suit jacket. "How could she? I didn't tell anyone where I was going, and she'd never guess."

The evidence of the lady on Tink's doorstep says otherwise.

There was a time when Tink would have reveled in making a grown-up pound and pound at her door. There was a time when she could have barricaded herself in the cottage for weeks, surviving on alcohol and pure spite. But she was old, and she was tired, and she wanted this woman to go away before she alerted the town to the fact that an immortal fairy was squatting at the Darling residence.

"I'm letting her in," says Tink. "If you want, you can hide in the closet."

Hope, now in only a bra and the skirt, kicks the suit jacket into the open door of the closet and then follows it. There is the sound of rummaging as she works to make space, and then the door closes. Tink takes a deep breath and then opens her door.

"Hello," she says, smiling broadly. "How may I help you?"

Hope's mother's jeans are tight and too youthful, with jewels sewn onto the pockets; her shirt is too low and reveals cleavage bolstered by a pink pushup bra Tink can see at the edges of the neckline. Yet there is this hardness, underneath, that makes her hair and her glasses and her nails even more ridiculous because it's all a show. She surveys the empty space behind Tink, probably looking for signs of her daughter.

"My name is Jennifer Bain," Hope's mother says. She slides the sunglasses down the bridge of her nose with the tip of one of her red fingernails. "I'm looking for my daughter, Hope."

"Sorry, what do you hope?" Tink asks. She tries to make her face look as blank as possible.

"No." Mrs. Bain takes a sharp breath in. She seems on the verge of anger. The emotion doesn't suit her; from her appearance, she is the kind of woman who likes to let men buy her drinks and then laugh vapidly at all of their jokes. "Her name is Hope."

"I don't know anyone by that name," says Tink with a shrug.

Again, Mrs. Bain takes a deep breath. Then she points, with her eyes, at something down to Tink's right. "Then why are her boots in your living room?"

Tink steps aside, and Mrs. Bain enters her home. Immediately, the whole room smells like vanilla and lavender. She kicks off her pink sandals at the door, and Tink wonders if she came right from Cabo.

"Alright, Hope," Mrs. Bain calls, in a way that says that she's done this exact thing many times before. "Come out, young lady, before I have to find you."

There is more rummaging, and then Hope trips and falls out of the closet. She catches herself, which is good because Tink doesn't rush to help her—she can't anyway, since she is strictly forbidden from using her wings with an adult present. But the real reason is that adults make Tink so nervous she feels paralyzed around them. From the fairy world to Neverland to the Darling mansion, all of Tink's homes have been blissfully parent-free. Now that a real parent has stepped into her house, she can barely move her hand to close the door.

"Why are you half-naked?" Mrs. Bain asks Hope. Her sunglasses are still perched low on her nose, and her pink lips are pursed.

"What do you care?" Hope asks. She doesn't seem interested in putting on a shirt, and in fact, seems proud of the fact that she's standing in the middle of Tink's living room in a bra and skirt.

"What do I care? I'm your mother."

Hope rolls her eyes, which is just what Tink would have done. "You didn't seem like my mother when you left me alone on Christmas to go to Cabo with Brian."

"Jesus, Hope." Finally, Mrs. Bain takes off her sunglasses and tucks one of the temples into her cleavage. "I'm an adult. You're an adult. I told you about this trip three months ago, and you agreed that you'd be okay spending the holidays with your aunt."

"I said 'Sure, I'll just fly to California and do goat yoga with Aunty Millie for Christmas instead of spending it at home with you.' That was obviously sarcasm."

"Well excuse me for not picking up on your snark." Mrs. Bain has taken her sunglasses back out of her cleavage and is waving them around for emphasis. "I should have known that when you said 'sure,' you meant 'I'm actually going to buy a plane ticket on your credit card, then not use that plane ticket, then fly to New York, and then spend Christmas with a homeless tomboy.'"

Tink opens her mouth to fire a counterattack, but no words come out.

"She's not homeless," says Hope. "You're literally standing in her home. And so what if she's a tomboy? I like tomboys."

"Oh, I know." Mrs. Bain puts her glasses on her head, and her pushed-back bangs reveal a line of earrings on each ear. "You've dated so many in the past year that I've had to start identifying them by the color of their flannel shirts instead of their names. What's the point?" She looks at Tink, who is currently wearing a green plaid shirt. "Green shirt will just be replaced by purple shirt next week."

Tink feels a sudden pull in her stomach, and she thinks of Wendy—and of the kind of mother that Wendy would have been. She thinks of little Andrew Bain, his face pressed against the glass waiting for his Fairy Princess to appear so that he can open the window and let her in. How time has erased him from Tink's memory, and yet how quickly she can call him back. Though Tink only spent a few years with him, she knows her little pacifist would have hated hearing Hope and Mrs. Bain fighting like this.

Do something, a voice says.

Wendy's voice.

"At least they wear age-appropriate clothes," says Hope. "I can't say the same for—"

"That's enough, both of you." Tink steps between them, though both women are taller than her and can probably just see each other over her head. She fights the urge to bolt. "I'm not especially experienced in the whole mother-daughter thing, but from what I can tell, Hope, you're actually upset that your mom moved on so soon after your dad died. You still need her to be there for you, and she's off in Cabo getting a tan and drinking margaritas. Is that right?"

"About sums it up," says Hope.

"Great. And Mrs. Bain, it sounds like you're trying to move on by . . . uh . . . " *Be polite, Tink.* " . . . going back to your fun pre-marriage days. You want to enjoy yourself so that you can take your mind off your dead husband. Right?"

"Not the words I would have used," says Mrs. Bain. "But yes. I guess."

"Perfect. So here's my proposal: Let Hope stay here for a few more days, during which you can enjoy your time with your boyfriend. Then meet her back home for Christmas and spend some time with her, because she's your daughter and she needs you." Tink can't believe the words coming out of her mouth. Has Wendy possessed her? She needs to get out of that stifling room. "And by the time you come back together, you'll both have had some time to think about how to be better to each other than you're being right now. What do you think? Can you both do that?"

Mrs. Bain and Hope just look at each other.

"Take some time to decide," says Tink. Her legs start to shake. She needs to be in open air. "But when I get back here in ten minutes, at least one of you better be gone."

Without waiting for a reply, she runs out the door and slams it behind her.

CHAPTER THIRTY-FIVE

Then

AFTER TINK DECIDED TO TAKE PETER back to the real world, the only obstacle left was convincing Peter to leave his treehouse. Tink marched back into his room and opened all of the curtains. Dust floated in the air; fruit flies danced around long-forgotten glasses of juice. The room was like a tomb—but she was going to raise Peter Pan from the dead.

"Get up," Tink instructed.

"Mmm." Peter rolled over and covered his face. "Come back tomorrow, Tink."

Tink grabbed the covers and yanked them off, revealing Peter's gangly body cramped on the too-small bed, like a fox in a stolen badger sett. He clutched his legs closer to his chest.

"You're going to get out of this bed whether you like it or not," said Tink, and she went over to the sink and filled up a mug with water.

"Go away," Peter moaned.

"I'll give you to the count of three, and then I'm dumping this water on your head. One." She took a step toward the bed. "Two." Closer she went. "Three."

At the last second, as the stream of water hovered on the lip of the mug, Peter sprang out of his bed. Before he could find another reclining spot—the sofa, perhaps, or maybe the floor—Tink grabbed him by the shoulders and shook him.

"Listen to me," she said, as Peter's teeth rattled, "you are Peter Pan. Father figure to the Lost Boys, love of Wendy Darling. You have a child, and you are not going to abandon it the way your parents abandoned you. Like it or not, you have a responsibility to that baby. Do you hear me? Do you hear me, Peter?"

Peter's face was blank as Tink shook and shook, but then it warped into something like a smile.

"Wendy," he said softly. "I remember Wendy."

There was no time for talk. Peter sprang to the window and pushed off the ledge; Tink followed him, sprinkling fairy dust on his back so that he didn't face plant in front of the Lost Boys. Up they soared, back through the hole, with Lost Boys whooping below them in enthusiasm.

"Tell me everything," Peter said, and Tink started at the beginning. There once was a girl named Wendy Darling . . .

* * *

WHEN THEY ARRIVED IN NEW YORK, Tink was surprised to find that in place of the fallen leaves and light snows, there were spring flowers in startling bouquets of pink and yellow everywhere on the Darling property. As they landed, she put her hand down and ran her fingers on the heads of the hydrangea bushes, taking loose petals with her by the fistful. Peter didn't seem to notice the change of scenery; then again, he probably didn't remember the Darling house at all.

Tink had tried her best to paint a picture of a happy relationship with Wendy, leaving out any mention of herself or the trouble she'd caused. She'd told Peter about the time he danced with Wendy, and that time in the woods, and he didn't ask how she knew. She'd told him about the night he left Wendy, and why, and what to say to make it all better. He'd nodded, and though Tink wasn't sure he could win his girl back, she was confident he at least remembered who she was.

When Tink and Peter knocked on the door, Wendy was the one to open it—or rather, the wide, round, beach-balled Wendy, whose shoulders strained back against the weight of her midsection. She wore a gown, not the midnight blue dress Tink remembered but a ruched black dress that went to her knees. Her eyes, upon seeing her visitors, went wide.

"Wendy?" Peter asked, and Tink wished her name sounded less like a question. Didn't he recognize the love of his life?

"Very funny," Tink said. She gave a fake laugh. "Why don't you tell *Wendy* what you came here to say?"

"Right." Peter removed his hat and wrung it in his hands. "Wendy. I . . . Well, I . . . "

Thumping came from behind Wendy, and then Michael forced his face past Wendy's girth. "Peter?" he asked, amazed.

"Oh. Hello . . . " Peter seemed to be struggling. The boy had not been part of Tink's review of events.

"Michael," Tink hinted.

"Michael." Peter hesitated. "I'm sorry, have we met?"

Wendy and Michael stared at Peter in a way that made Tink's hopes sink—in a way that said, *Has Peter gone mad?*

"I'm sorry," Wendy said. Her eyes teared up. "I can't do this right now . . . I'm about to go to the dance . . . I just . . . "

"The dance?" Tink looked around her, confirming there really were spring flowers. "Didn't that happen in December?"

"Not the Winter Ball," said Wendy. "My prom. It's May, Tink. Isn't that why you're dressed like that?"

Tink looked down and realized she was still wearing her uniform. "Of course it is," she said quickly, "I forgot all about it when Peter told me he desperately needed to talk to you. To say something very important. Isn't that right, Peter?"

Naturally, Peter chose that minute to stay silent. He looked like an old man with Alzheimer's the way he kept whipping his head back and forth, hoping for something to make sense.

A car came down the driveway, the crunch of gravel and tire treads saving Tink and Peter from conversation. When the car turned in front of them, Tink recognized the broad shoulders and blue blazer of the fresh-faced youth. The windows were down, and the boy was humming along to one of the worst songs Tink had ever heard—as if computers had decided to make a digital imitation of a human song. She wrinkled her nose and thought of Peter's flute, accompanied by Lost

Boys on the harmonica, banjo, and drums. Now that was music.

"Why is Paul here?" Tink asked. "Don't tell me—"

"The limo's right behind us," Paul said through the open window. "Wow, Wendy you look great."

"Thank you, Paul, that's very generous of you." Wendy tried to pass Tink and Peter, but Peter grabbed her arm.

"Wendy, wait." Peter rubbed his forehead, as though thinking hurt him. "I may not know who this idiot is, and I may not know Michael, but I know you. I'm sorry that I left, but I'm back." He moved closer and whispered, "I need you. And you need me, too."

Maybe everything would have been fine if he hadn't looked down at her belly right at that moment. But he did, and by the way Wendy's eyes narrowed, Tink knew she'd seen it too.

"I need you?" Wendy said, much louder than Peter had been talking. "I *need* you? You've been gone for months. You've missed doctor's appointments, ultrasounds, heartbeats. You've missed everything." She pulled her arm out of his grasp. "Maybe I did think I needed you, once, but that was a lifetime ago."

She tried to step off of the porch, but Peter grabbed her again, throwing her off balance. She teetered on the edge of a step, a boulder on the verge of rolling down a mountain, and then Tink sped to catch her with just the slightest flick of her wings. Wendy fell into her arms, and then Wendy righted herself before Tink had the embarrassment of giving in under the weight. They stood close to each other but didn't separate, and Tink stared into those brown eyes, so full of the emotion Wendy hid from everyone else, and felt like crying for the part she'd played in all of this.

"Wendy, I . . . "

Wendy leaned in and whispered in Tink's ear. For as long as she lives, she will not forget those words. "I love you. But I need you to leave now, and to take Peter with you. Do you understand?"

Tink nodded. She wished she had time to say everything in her heart, but Paul had leapt out of his car at the sight of the limo and was now pulling her away.

"Wendy!" Peter called, but she and Paul disappeared into the door of the long black car. Through the tinted windows, all Tink could see was that Wendy had turned away from them and didn't look back.

CHAPTER THIRTY-SIX

"Forgetfulness"

Excerpt from *Neverland: A History*

CONSIDERING THE DANGERS OF A FORGETFULNESS spell (see later chapter on "Mermaids" for one example), readers may wonder why we bothered enchanting Neverland in the first place. The Lost Boys were brought to the island as babies; what difference did it make whether they remembered those first days of life?

The truth is that the forgetfulness spell was never intended to make the boys forget their homes on Earth—that was just a side effect. The real reason the Lost Boys had to be enchanted was that the human brain cannot bear the burden of immortality—eventually, the years upon years of life put on them like dirt onto a coffin will break them under their weight, and they will go insane.

How do we know this?

Because the Lost Boys were not the first humans to enter the Magical Realm.

The first human to enter the Magical Realm was a man named Jeremiah Latch.

A long time ago—before I blossomed, even—a visiting King brought the Fairy Queen of that time a unique gift: a human storyteller named Jeremiah Latch. Latch had been abducted during the King's recent visit to Earth, when Latch accidentally charmed the ruler with a creative retelling of Cain and Abel that made the King cry. Little did Latch know that his hooded listener was actually a visiting royal, or that fifteen minutes of talking in a town square would earn him immortality.

At first, Latch enjoyed his new life. He drank gallons of sap a day, told stories all night, and had the undivided attention of an entire tree full of sprites. Eventually, however, his mind tired in a way his body never could.

He stopped tasting the sap.

He stopped enjoying the stories.

The fairies drove him mad with all of their fawning and pleading for *Just one more tale!* He had to escape the Fairy Realm—but as my readers well know, without wings, Jeremiah was powerless to change his fate. He couldn't even die, watched as he was by several of the Queen's guards.

So Jeremiah Latch did the only thing he knew would earn him the death he so desperately craved.

He murdered our poor Queen.

It is said that when the guards took him away, he began spinning tales the way he hadn't in years. It is said that those stories made Jeremiah Latch cry, so long had he been without enjoyment of them.

It is said that even on the day they removed his head, his lips were the last part of him to move.

CHAPTER THIRTY-SEVEN

Now

WENDY'S VOICE HAS DISAPPEARED, BUT THAT doesn't mean she won't be back. Just knowing about her presence unnerves Tink, so she does what she always does when she feels unsettled: goes to the stump to chop firewood. Her splitting maul leans where she left it, against the trunk of a nearby tree, and after she puts on her gloves she swings it up to her shoulder and carries it to the stump. Then she retrieves a log from the pile and stands it up on the stump, which is just the right height to make her swings most effective. Her stove takes twenty-inch pieces, so she needs to reduce her logs to that size—though she would probably cut her wood anyway just to give her hands something to do.

"I didn't know people still chop wood." Hope has come up behind her, though she stays far enough away from Tink to avoid accidental injury.

"How else can I kill a few lifetimes?" Tink asks, and swings the maul up.

"Good point."

Tink feels like an executioner about to remove a head. She pauses, enjoying the power of a poised weapon, and then aims for a crack in the log. With a flick of her wrists, the maul goes down and makes impact, splitting the log like two continents dividing at a fault line. One summersaults off of the trunk, and the other teeters on the edge and then settles there.

"A clean break," says Tink. "But that one didn't even make a foot."

The furthest a piece of wood has ever flown was four feet, seven inches. Tink knows this because she measured it, and there is currently a gray rock in the exact place of collision. She considers telling Hope about her little contest, but then decides against it. Her life will only sound more pathetic than it already seems.

"So what happened with your mom?" Tink asks.

Hope sits down on another stump at the edge of the clearing and slides her hands between her thighs. Now that day is turning to night, the temperature has dropped significantly; it will probably snow again. "She went back to Cabo," Hope finally says. She doesn't sound as enthusiastic as Tink would have expected.

"And are you going to be together for Christmas?"

"So it would seem." Hope pauses. Then, "Thanks for that, by the way."

"Anytime. But you don't seem thrilled about the idea anymore."

"I know." As though she, too, feels anxious, Hope gets up and retrieves a log for Tink. "I got what I wanted, and now I'm not sure why I wanted it. Mom has moved on, and I'm stuck in the past . . . but I don't really want to leave it. Do you know what I mean?"

Tink raises her eyebrows. “I think you know I do.”

She chops a few more logs, though there is a pile of firewood so tall and wide that it could feed a hundred fires that winter. Then, when her muscles have relaxed in the way her mind cannot, she sits down on the trunk and pulls out her flask.

“You drink a lot,” Hope points out.

“Well, you stick your nose in other people’s business a lot,” says Tink. Then she toasts Hope and makes a big show of her next gulp.

“Well, you’re squatting on my land.”

“Well, you wouldn’t have any land to speak of if I hadn’t taken care of it for all of these years.”

Hope grins. Then she extends her hand, and Tink screws the cap back on the flask and tosses it to her. Snow has begun to fall again in fat flakes that look like little suns burning in Hope’s sunset-red hair. Tink thinks of the first time Peter saw snow, and how he called the flakes “rain crystals” as he darted through the air catching them on his palm. She thinks of how he looked then, dusted by ice, like he was freezing over. A frozen boy, a forever boy, and yet now Tink wipes those same flakes off of his gravestone.

“Tink?”

“What?” Tink shakes her head.

“I asked if you wanted more.” Hope sloshes the flask.

“Oh. No.” Tink has had enough; she has begun to slip through time again, and soon she won’t remember when she is. “Maybe we should get you inside.”

Hope grins at her. “Actually, I have a better idea.”

They pile the logs in a square, as though they're building a cabin. In the middle they put kindling. Tink retrieves a newspaper from her cabin and a lighter, which Hope uses to set the paper on fire. "Here we go," she says, and drops the burning ball into the center of the square. While Hope nurses the flames, Tink retrieves her chairs from the house and the rest of the coffee in thermoses that have long since lost their lids.

"Just in time," Hope says as the sun disappears beneath the horizon.

Back when Tink flew with Peter, they used to chase the sun around the earth. Their shadows would stretch behind them like very long capes, and when they flew in formation, their two black lines became one.

"Are you thinking about Wendy?" Hope asks.

"Peter, actually. He's always on my mind."

"Oh right, you never finished the story." Hope pauses and seems to be thinking. "From what I remember, Paul had just picked up Wendy from the Darling house and taken her to the prom. Did Peter go back to Neverland with you?"

Tink considers lying. She considers making up a new story, one in which Peter did turn away from the house and fly away to Neverland to start a new life. One in which she isn't the villain. But she doesn't have the energy to lie, and besides, what good would it do?

"No. He didn't go back."

Tink can't bring herself to go on, and Hope doesn't press. Instead, she moves her chair closer and leans her shoulder against Tink's, and then her head. Tink doesn't move; she can barely breathe.

"Listen, Hope," she finally gets out, "I can't—"

"I know, I know, you're still in love with both of them. But they're gone, Tink. Don't you want to move on?"

Tink wants to cry, but she laughs instead. The sound grates against the silence of the forest like a chainsaw at the bark of a tree.

"That's the funny part," she says, and now she finally is crying. "Wendy isn't dead."

CHAPTER THIRTY-EIGHT

Then

PETER AND TINK STOOD ON THE porch, with the limo gone and the door closed against them by Michael.

"I have to follow her," Peter said. Then he put out his arms. "Sprinkle your dust, quickly."

Tink took a deep breath. "You know I can't do that Peter," she said very quietly.

"What do you mean? You help me fly all the time." His eyes followed the limo.

"This is different, Peter. This is the real world, in daylight. It's against the rules."

"The rules?" Peter yelled. "Since when do you care about the rules?"

Tink didn't say anything. Even bad fairies had their limits, and besides, Wendy didn't want him to follow her. She'd specifically instructed Tink to take him away. Letting Peter go to the dance would only make things worse.

Peter must have realized that she wasn't going to give him any fairy dust, because his eyes went to the car in the driveway. In his rush, Paul had left his keys in the ignition. Leave it to Paul to forget a neon green keychain, thought Tink.

"No way," she said.

"I have to." He walked down the steps and just stood there looking at the car.

"But you can't drive. Peter, did you hear me?" Tink waved a hand in front of his face. "You can't drive."

Later, Tink will think back on this moment so many times that it wears down, like nervous fingers twisting a napkin to shreds. She will think back on Peter, on the way that his eyes glazed and his shoulders shook from manic energy, but she will not remember what happens right afterward. Somehow he slipped away from her, and by the time she realized that he was inside of the car, he had already locked the door.

"Peter?" Tink yelled. She pounded on the window with her fist until it hurt. "Peter?"

Inside the car, Peter was figuring out what to do. He eventually turned the key, sending the engine roaring; a minute later, he figured out the gear shift. Tink thought about the time that Peter had proclaimed he would tame the cranky old rhinoceros, Old Oh, that terrorized the Lost Boys whenever they wanted a Never fruit from the sweetest tree. How worried she had been when Old Oh bucked and kicked, and when he had run at the tree with full force in an attempt to crash Peter off of his back. Peter had held on that time, but the tree had been ruined by Old Oh's blow.

"Stop!" she screamed, but Peter floored the petal and peeled down the driveway. *Screw the rules*, Tink thought, and flew after him, pushing her wings forward even as they protested. They had already flown her from Neverland less than ten minutes before, and they were spent. *Go, go, go,* she urged, and for a while longer, they obeyed.

Peter quickly caught up with the limo, which had only turned onto the main road and gone a little while down the straight path to Wendy's school. He honked, and Wendy's head appeared out of the sunroof.

"Peter, what are you doing?" she yelled. Then she looked at Tink, who was flying beside the car, and her mouth fell open.

"I need to talk to you," Peter called out the window to her.

Wendy blinked a few times. Then she rubbed her eyes. Tink smiled sheepishly, and Wendy's eyes went wide. Tink recognized belief when she saw it.

"Tell the limo to stop," Peter demanded.

Maybe Wendy didn't hear him; maybe she was too distracted by Tink's flying to give him a second thought. Whatever the reason, she didn't stop the limo, and Peter, in his panic, decided to veer into the left lane. He probably planned to cut the limo off, even if it meant putting his car directly in the driver's way—only the car coming from the opposite direction had different ideas.

"Peter, no!" Tink screamed, but it was too late.

Peter's car accordioned into the oncoming car, which spun just enough to hit the front of the limousine. Wendy was thrown from the sunroof onto the grass that divided the road from the forest, which turned out to be for the best because the limo drove straight into the trees.

Tink knew just by looking at what remained of the car that Peter was gone, so she did the only thing she could: she went numb. Wendy was still alive according to her moans, so Tink flew to her side and lifted her head onto her forearm. Blood trickled from a wound on her head. Another driver, a mother with young children calling out in the back of her van, ran over with her cell phone and dialed 9-1-1.

"Stay with me," Tink whispered to Wendy.

She clutched her hand, and Wendy squeezed it once.

Then she was gone.

* * *

"ARE YOU WENDY'S SISTER?"

A doctor in a white coat was looking down at Tink from high above her. Tink had fallen asleep in the waiting room chair—a miraculous feat considering the hard metal was barely softened by a red plastic cover, but then again, it had been ten hours. The room smelled like cleaning spray and bad coffee.

"Yes. I'm Tink Darling," Tink lied as she rubbed her eyes, still struggling to grasp where she was, and when.

The doctor nodded. Maybe he doubted her story—after all, Wendy and Tink looked nothing alike—but he apparently wasn't confident enough to call her bluff.

"We've stabilized her, for now. She's expressed to us that she would like us to remove the baby, who seems unharmed, so we're planning to start the surgery in a few minutes. I thought you might want to say your goodbyes now, just in case."

"I don't understand—"

"Wendy is not going to make it," the doctor said. "Her organs have already begun to fail."

The doctor continued to talk, but Tink didn't hear him. *Not going to make it.* The words echoed and reechoed. I can't lose them both, Tink thought.

"Do you want to see her now?" The doctor asked.

"Yes," Tink said, distracted. She needed to save Wendy—she needed to do something right, after everything she'd done wrong.

She needed to get Wendy to Neverland.

As soon as the doctor showed her to Wendy's room, Tink slipped inside and then closed the door behind her. She had minutes, if that. Wendy was laid out on the hospital bed, too much like a corpse on a metal table, and a shiver went up Tink's spine. Her hair had been pulled back, away from her face, revealing stitched wounds and bruises on one side. A monitor beeped out her pulse. Liquids poured into her from bags on metal hangers.

Hopefully, at least one of them was a painkiller.

"Tink?" Wendy whispered.

"I'm here," Tink said.

"You flew," Wendy said. "That was real, wasn't it?"

"Yes, it was real."

"I thought so."

Tink was running out of time. She turned to the tray of instruments prepped for Wendy's surgery and sifted through the cold metal objects until she found a scalpel and needle. Then she gulped.

"What are you doing?" Wendy asked.

Tink stripped out of the top half of her uniform and raised her wings. How beautiful they were, even in that darkly lit room, like a stained-glass window in an otherwise somber steeple.

Deep breath, Tink.

She raised the scalpel and then brought it down once, twice, over and over again. Images flooded her mind—times when she and Peter flew over Neverland, times when she was just a new fairy learning how to navigate a thermal, times that were over now, at least between Tink and those wings. She thought of the tree in the center of the Home Under the Ground, which every morning one of the Lost Boys must chop down just to have the tree spring up again from its trunk. The pain was like nothing Tink had ever felt before, and if she weren't immortal, she would have fainted. Finally, with a snap, her wings fell away from her body and onto the floor. Tink took up the twitching wings and carried them to the bed.

"Come on," she said, and lifted Wendy up just enough to reveal her back through the tied hospital gown.

"I don't understand . . . What are you . . . Tink?" Wendy leaned forward onto her belly, probably more from exhaustion than helpfulness.

"Everything is going to be okay," Tink said as she raised the needle. "I promise."

Quickly, she began to sew.

* * *

Later, they would find the paperwork for baby Andrew on Wendy's tray—only Wendy, herself, was gone. They would say it was impossible, that no one with her injuries could be moved, let alone walk out herself. They would make rumors about her, a ghost named Wendy who haunted the emergency ward spooking drunk teens and stealing supplies out of the cabinets so that nurses would curse her under their breaths.

Or at least that's how Tink imagined things went.

By then, she was trudging through the forest on her way back to the Darling house, a path of green drops of blood in her wake.

CHAPTER THIRTY-NINE

"Council Involvement"

Excerpt from *Neverland: A History*

THE COUNCIL ORIGINALLY INTENDED TO SET up an extensive network of embassies on the island, but soon after Neverland reached an equilibrium, war broke out. We did not abandon Neverland—after all, our emissary Tinker Bell had a close eye on the goings-on of Peter Pan and the other inhabitants—but we also did not necessarily act the part of responsible founders. And by the time the war was over, Tinker Bell and Peter were gone.

This is not to say that it was hard to track them down. In fact, finding Tinker Bell on Earth was as easy as waiting for the sun to set and looking for the telltale twinkle of fairy wings among the otherwise dull lights of humanity.

However, just because I found her did not mean that I immediately made her aware of my presence.

Tinker Bell had an obstinate personality—that was, after all, the reason that we chose her—and I knew that ordering her and Peter to Neverland would not work on either of them. They were like two whales intent on beaching themselves up on the shore, and sending them back to the water would only result in them washing up again the next day. So I resolved to watch from a distance, spectator to a drama that I had accidentally produced. After all, I had been the one to select Tink for the job; I had been the one to send her to Neverland; I had been the one assigned to guarantee that the leader of the Lost

Boys was where he belonged, in a treehouse in his Home Under the Ground, with Tink by his side.

Watching this drama unfold, however, proved more difficult than I had originally anticipated.

Not only did Tinker Bell fail to convince Peter Pan to return to Neverland, but it was obvious that she had developed feelings for the same human as Peter. Her affection fascinated me as a historian, but horrified me as a member of my race. I needed to observe her further, but since I could not go undetected in the Darling house, I could witness only what went on outside. I was there the day Tink fled to the cabin, and the day John taught the others how to dance, and the day that Tinker Bell saved Michael from the creek.

I knew, as I watched her warm Michael with her own clothes, that Tink would soon be forced to make a very difficult choice: leave then with Peter, or grow too attached to her new family to ever leave again.

Here I must pause to make a confession that has haunted me for many years. It is a confession that I have made to Tinker Bell, but to no others on the Council or on the royal throne. Even now, I have couched my confession in a chapter titled, innocently enough, "Council Involvement," when really, "Council Involvement—or Lack Thereof" would have been more accurate.

You see, though I was there every day that Peter and Tinker Bell spent with the Darlings, I was not there on the day that Peter died.

Although it was my duty to watch them and make sure that this time, unlike the last, they actually stayed where they belonged, like any servant asked to guard the same post for too long, I grew bored. Yes, dear reader, even I, historian and all-around professional observer, could not stand the monotony of watching the entrance to the Home Under the Ground day in and day out. We fairies may be immortal, but we still want to enjoy our years the same as any other being.

Alright.

I must write this quickly, like removing an arrow from a recent wound.

On that day, that fateful day, I was sunning my wings on the soft sand of Mermaids' Lagoon.

I know, I know. Of all the places to be during a crisis, a beach is by far the worst. Not only does it show negligence, but also indulgence—two traits unbefitting a Council member like myself.

Be that as it may, that is the truth. Peter was dying on Earth, and I was drying off after a swim.

By the time the Lost Boys came searching the island for Tink and Peter, an hour had passed. I knew exactly where they had gone, and though I urged my wings forward like two steeds pulling a carriage, I was too late. Perhaps I could have prevented the accident; perhaps I might have, with Tink's help, been able to restrain Peter long enough for him to regain his senses.

Perhaps I could have changed Tink's fate.

But I hadn't. And I couldn't.

And Peter Pan was dead.

I tell you all of this now not just to ease my own guilt, but to explain what happened next. Tink was right to suspect my presence, for in fact, I never left her side again. Even during the times she entered her cottage to sleep, I hovered in the shadows, watching over her as she restlessly battled her own guilt. Once, I even kissed her sweating forehead, and she found peace then, if only for a few minutes.

After a while, the Council called me back to the Fairy Realm. I'd convinced them that Tink was no threat to our species as long as she had removed her wings and secluded herself from the outside world, but therefore, they saw no purpose in my sentineling a lost fairy.

For the first time in my long life, I ignored a direct command.

Then I tracked down Hope Darling.

CHAPTER FORTY

Now

"WAIT." HOPE SITS AS FAR AWAY from Tink as she can. "You're telling me that my grandmother has been alive this whole time? And you hid that from me?"

"Hope, I—"

"Were you ever going to tell me?"

Tink looks at the fire and says, "I don't know."

Hope stands up and begins to pace. "I don't understand. None of this makes any sense. If you can grow your wings back anytime you want, and Wendy is there, then why haven't you gone back to Neverland?"

"What would be the point?" Tink asks morosely. "Wendy won't remember me, and neither will the Lost Boys."

Hope looks at her hard. "Bullshit," she says.

"Fine. It's not just that. I don't . . . " She tries to find the words.

"Deserve to be happy?"

Tink nods.

"So what? Most people don't. We've all messed things up; we've all hurt people. Hell, my mom just had to fly here from Cabo because I ghosted my aunt to come hang out here for the holidays. But you think that makes her love me any less?"

Tink shakes her head. "That's different. She's your mom—"

"And Wendy is the love of your life." Hope comes over to Tink and shakes her shoulders. "Wake up, Tink. You might be immortal, but a fish without water is just dinner."

Tink stands up fast, overturning her chair. "What did you just say?"

"It's just something my dad used to—"

But Tink doesn't hear her. She is back in Neverland, on a boulder, talking to Andalain. She is back in Peter's room, reminding him of who he is—and who he could be. *We're so similar,* Tink thinks, only instead of six months she's been gone for almost forty years.

But she can't stay away anymore.

You are Tinker Bell, guardian of Lost Boys, love of Wendy Darling. You are not going to hide from the repercussions of what you've done. Like it or not, you have a responsibility to Wendy. Do you hear me? Do you hear me, Tink?

The voice sounds like Wendy, and yet it is Peter—and most of all, it is Tink's voice, because they have all been Tinker Bell all along.

"I have to . . . "

"Go," Hope urges. "I like you and everything, but I'll get over you, I promise."

"Thanks?" Tink says. Then, after a minute, "I guess I feel the same way about you."

Though she can't really see Hope because of the descending darkness, she thinks she sees her smile. Then

Tink is up, up, up through the trees and over the forest that leads away from the Darling house and straight on till morning.

* * *

When Tink arrives in Neverland, a thick mist shrouds the island. Her shoes are gone; her jacket is windbeaten and soaked. By heart, she soars down into the fog and aims straight until she stops abruptly and points her toes, feeling the leaves of the Never trees against her bare feet. From there she veers right and finds the hole in the canopy, then drops a hundred feet below ground.

The Home Under the Ground is like a light fading off, the coals of the nightly bonfire cooling to dark. Most of the Lost Boys have fallen asleep around the embers, legs curled to their chests, thumbs in their mouths, soft expressions hinting at sweet dreams. Some of them babble, the babies they once were reemerging in their heavy slumber. Tink thinks of cats, the way they can curl up and fall asleep anywhere.

Tink lands far enough outside of their circle to evade notice and orients herself. Not much has changed since her departure forty years before, though there are a few new treehouses, haphazard compared to the solid structures Peter built. One even has a sheet for a roof, strung over two pieces of siding that, judging by the gun port, came from a wrecked ship. Tink wonders if there are pirates in Neverland again, and if so, whether they have managed to extract any of the gold from Mermaids' Lagoon. Then again, judging by the fact that part of a ship has made it to the Lost Boys, she doubts it very much.

Now that she is back, she is not sure where to go. There is a lamp burning in the window of Peter's treehouse, and she wonders which Lost Boy has been put in charge and given his quarters. Big Mitch, who could eat a hundred Never fruits before getting sick? Hairy Harrison, who had always lit the bonfire in Peter's absence? Sammy Sam, who had once wrestled a boar to the ground and killed it with one arm?

She wants to find Wendy, but entering Neverland without paying respects to the chief is like visiting England and not paying your respects to the Queen. At best, they would think her a foreigner; at worst, an assailant. Like the mermaids, the Lost Boys could be dangerous when provoked. Tink mounted the stairs to Peter's house, noting that the steps had been swept clean of Never tree leaves and the door had a fresh coat of paint, and knocked twice, three knocks per time, as the Lost Boys did when sounding out their code.

"Coming," someone says. The voice is familiar, and Tink feels Wendy coming in the physiological reaction of her entire body, from trembling hands to shuffling feet, even before she sees her. The door opens, revealing the girl that Tink once knew—and yet this girl is an entirely different girl, too. This girl wears a boar skin dress, and slippers woven from reeds. She has a flower tucked behind one ear. Her pale skin is sun-toasted and freckled. When she moves, her steps are chest-first, the way Peter used to strut.

"Wendy?" Tink asks.

Wendy blinks a few times. "Who are you?" she asks. Then, before Tink can answer, Wendy disappears into the room.

"Uh . . . Wendy?" Tink calls, but Wendy doesn't reply. Unsure what to do, Tink follows her into the room, which is lit by a single beeswax candle on the table. It takes her a few minutes to orient herself, since Wendy has rearranged the furniture. There are other differences: a bouquet of flowers by the bed, a basket with dried fruit sweetening the air, a painting in a wooden frame where Peter's crocodile tooth used to hang on a piece of twine.

Wendy is in front of the painting, inspecting it. Tink finds this behavior incredibly odd, but when she comes to stand next to Wendy and looks at the painting, she realizes why this particular item has caught the girl's attention. It is, unquestioningly, a painting of Tinker Bell. She wears her uniform instead of her flannel shirt, and her shoes are dainty slippers instead of bare feet, and her hair is longer as required by the royal guard in order to promote the flirtatious behavior of tucking the ends behind her attractively pointy ears, but still.

"I painted this," Wendy says in a way that makes the statement sound like a question. "I don't remember when . . . It was before . . . before now."

Wendy looks the way Alzheimer's patients look in the real world when someone tries to explain where they are—*when* they are. Tink knows well that time in Neverland is like the water of Mermaids' Lagoon, clear when cupped in your hand but always slipping through your fingers.

"It's a beautiful painting," Tink says.

"Thanks." Wendy nods her head demurely. Then she points to something in the right corner, some letters that Tink assumed was a signature. "It says . . . Well, I'm not sure."

Tink looks at Wendy and realizes from her squinted eyes that Wendy does not remember how to read.

Tink gets up very close and sounds out the words. "'Turn me over.'"

They each take a side of the frame and lift it off of the peg. Carefully they set the painting on the ground, and sure enough, there is more black ink on the back. Considering there are no brushes or pens in Neverland and none of the boys there even know how to write, Tink wonders how Wendy even found an implement.

"What does it say?" Wendy asks.

Even after all of this time, Tink has never learned how to read more than very simple words. Wendy must have known that, because she only wrote the simple ones, and Tink is able to piece the longer words together through clues.

"This is Tinker Bell. She saved your life. You are in love with her, but you don't remember. When she tells you her story, be kind."

Tears blur Tink's vision, but she has read the entire message anyway and so she looks away. Though she is standing next to Wendy after all of this time, the real Wendy, the Wendy she knew and fell in love with, exists only in those words.

"What does she—I mean 'I'—mean by 'be kind'?"

Tink puts her finger down to touch the ink and traces her finger over the words. She can almost see Wendy bent over the woven canvas, furiously penning her message before she forgets her own memories. Wendy, always so practical, and stubborn in her own way. What would she think of the fact that Tink considers keeping the past to herself? Of telling Wendy that she has no idea, and that maybe the old Wendy was deranged? What would she think of the way Tink wants to start again, as a clean slate, so that she can finally get the happy ending she's dreamed of but never deserved?

"Do you have cocoa, or maybe some Never fruit tea?" Tink asks as she turns away from the writing. She hasn't lived for all of these years just to make the same mistakes. "It's a long story, and I want to tell it right."

CHAPTER FORTY-ONE

"Current Leadership"

Excerpt from *Neverland: A History*

TINK AND WENDY BECAME, BY UNOFFICIAL agreement, the first rulers to share leadership of the band of Lost Boys. During their reign, which is still ongoing and the source of the funding for this extensive history, Neverland has been transformed from a wild island under temporary truce to a thriving community known for its mermaid glass, Kandallanian rugs, and Never tree syrup that has been collected, boiled, and filtered by the Lost Boys.

What happened between Tinker Bell and Wendy that night in Peter's treehouse has never been uncovered. We know about the painting, and the message on the back, but not how Tink won Wendy's heart or how, after so many years of loneliness and pain, Tinker Bell was able to move on from the terrible tragedy that weighed so heavily on her small shoulders.

However, it does not take much of an imaginative act to picture the two of them together, hunched over the little wooden table, talking through Tink's many secrets until Wendy, sweet girl that she is, put a hand on her arm and told her gently that everything was going to be okay. It does not take much of a leap to think that when they touched, the sparks that had flown between them and been suppressed for the sake of a brash boy with a careless heart who nonetheless had loved Wendy until the day he died.

What we do know, from the Lost Boys with better memories, is that Tink and Wendy emerged into the early morning looking tired but triumphant. They had faced their demons, and they had been reborn. Little Samuel tells of the way the two girls—or, one might say, women—held hands as they walked past the sleeping bodies just blinking awake at the sound of their footsteps, and how they mounted a stump on the far side of the Home Under the Ground and began to sing like a bird, the way Peter Pan had sung many years ago. Sammy Sam tells of the chorus of Lost Boys who joined them, even though they did not recall why they felt so strongly that singing was a thing that had to be done or who had ever taught them the skill of gathering their breath, throwing their head back, and sending their voices up through the hole at the top of the tunnel, through the Never trees, and into the dawning day.

EPILOGUE

Later

EVERY YEAR, GODMOTHER ANNE MAKES THE long journey from the fairy realm to upstate New York to check on Hope Darling. She is late this time, but she forgives herself this slip—trade routes for the increased production of Never tree syrup must be negotiated with care, she justifies, and besides, she could not leave the boys to themselves, not even on their best behavior, not with Wendy and Tink gone on their mysterious adventure. No, they are not ready for that much responsibility yet. Luckily, the leaves are still red and healthy on the stem, and Godmother Anne alights on her usual branch a safe distance from the house, shielded by thick boughs.

The morning watch passes without human incident. Godmother Anne does have other visitors: a curious fox that she scares away from the base of the tree; a family of four deer that munch grass and watch her with the wide black marbles of their wary eyes; a squirrel that learns quickly not to direct his anxious screeches in her direction. She naps. She runs through the planned export of a hundred crates of mermaid glass, looking for weaknesses in the supply chain. Oh, the responsibility of a budding economy—but here is Hope now, leaving the house in an oversized green flannel shirt, black leggings, and duck boots. Her hair is curly and wild. Could this be the same girl who used to tower over everyone on the busy streets of Atlanta with her arms crossed in warning?

"Coming?" Hope calls back into the house.

An eager face appears in the space between Hope and the door. "Can we?"

"Alright." Hope reaches back into the house and then leans over with a furry red coat for the girl. "But we're going to have to rake them all up again, okay?"

The girl is already racing down the steps. She was two when Hope brought her home last year, a toddler taking unsteady steps across the porch and then tripping her way across the yard, but now she is fast, almost flying, into the first pile of leaves. She begins a slow wade across the pile, keeping her arms stretched out for balance. "There's leaves in my boots!" she exclaims. "Lots of them!"

Hope shakes her head. "There better not be fleas in those leaves, Isabelle." But she is laughing, and soon she is taking pictures of the girl as she throws the leaves skyward.

"Did you hear that?" a voice says from somewhere nearby. "Do you think she named her Isabelle after me? Get it? Isa*belle*? Tinker *Bell*? Come on!"

Tink? Godmother Anne almost falls off the branch. Her wings snap open, steadying her until she finds her footing, and then quickly close. Sure enough, when she looks left and ahead about twenty feet, she spies a familiar green coat and boar skin dress amidst the red leaves and thick branches. The angle of their perch means that they cannot see Godmother Anne, but she can see them and hear them clearly. And when did they arrive? Was she asleep longer than she'd realized?

"Shhh," says Wendy. "You have to be quiet."

"I'm always quiet," says Tink in a slightly lower but just as audible tone. "I'm just happy for her, that's all."

"Me too." Wendy opens her mouth to say something else but then closes it.

"I'm sure she would want to meet you," Tink says. "When you're ready."

"I know." Wendy takes a deep breath. "I just wish I could remember . . . "

Branches rustle, and when Godmother Anne looks carefully, she thinks she sees Tink put her arm around Wendy. Poor girl. Poor, sweet, forgetful Wendy. Yes, the Fairy Queen has finally lifted the forgetfulness curse, but one cannot simply remember what one has forgotten—or, in Wendy's case, what one has wanted desperately to forget.

"Maybe next time," says Tink.

The two girls stay quiet as Isabelle darts out the other side of the pile and begins a game of tag with Hope. Then they dig out weeds in the garden, Hope with a spade and Isabelle with a matching plastic tool. Soon it is lunchtime, and after Hope and Isabelle go inside, a car appears. Godmother Anne knows Mrs. Bain well from her previous trips, as well as her boyfriend, Brian, who is inappropriately dressed for the weather in a tropical shirt and shorts.

Or perhaps they are leaving for another trip—a honeymoon, perhaps, judging by the sparkly new ring on Mrs. Bain's finger?

When Hope comes to the door again, she hugs her mother and then hesitates before shaking Brian's hand. They seem content. Godmother Anne is happy; after all, she was the one who sent Mrs. Bain the alert about the fraudulent charges on her credit card after Hope bought the ticket. A risk, that reunion—but a calculated one.

"Want to stay?" Tink asks Wendy.

"I think I'm ready to go see the graves," says Wendy. "We haven't ever gone, and I owe Peter that much."

"No." More rustling—probably Tink shaking her head, or perhaps wiping Wendy's cheek. "Trust me, after decades of feeling that way, I finally realized you don't owe anyone anything. Just live, Wendy. That's all."

A few minutes later, the girls fly off holding hands, just a blur and then a shadow in the clouds; Godmother Anne resists the urge to follow them. She has played her part, and she knows that when she leaves New York this time, it will be for good. She does not owe Tink or Wendy or Hope anything—not anymore.

ABOUT THE AUTHOR

Kelly Ann Jacobson is the author or editor of numerous published books, including *An Inventory of Abandoned Things,* winner of the Split/Lip Chapbook Contest, *Miranda* (2018, Storylandia!), *Three on the Bank* (2014, Storylandia!), and *Cairo in White* (2014, Musa Publishing). In addition, she has edited a number of anthologies via CreateSpace including *The Way to My Heart: An Anthology of Food-Related Romance* (2017), *Candlesticks and Daggers: An Anthology of Mixed-Genre Mysteries* (2016), and *Dear Robot: An Anthology of Epistolary Science Fiction* (2015). Her short fiction, poetry, and nonfiction has appeared in more than fifty journals and other publications, including *Monkeybicycle, Iron Horse Literary Review, Cleaver Magazine, Best Small Fictions 2020,* and *Daily Science Fiction.* Kelly received her PhD in Creative Writing from Florida State University, and teaches speculative fiction for Southern New Hampshire University's online MFA in creative writing. More information about her can be found at www.kellyannjacobson.com. She currently resides in Virginia.

RECENT AND FORTHCOMING BOOKS FROM THREE ROOMS PRESS

FICTION

Lucy Jane Bledsoe
No Stopping Us Now

Rishab Borah
The Door to Inferna

Meagan Brothers
Weird Girl and What's His Name

Christopher Chambers
Scavenger

Ron Dakron
Hello Devilfish!

Robert Duncan
Loudmouth

Michael T. Fournier
Hidden Wheel
Swing State

Aaron Hamburger
Nirvana Is Here

William Least Heat-Moon
Celestial Mechanics

Aimee Herman
Everything Grows

Kelly Ann Jacobson
Tink and Wendy

Jethro K. Lieberman
Everything Is Jake

Eamon Loingsigh
Light of the Diddicoy
Exile on Bridge Street

John Marshall
The Greenfather

Aram Saroyan
Still Night in L.A.

Stephen Spotte
Animal Wrongs

Richard Vetere
The Writers Afterlife
Champagne and Cocaine

Julia Watts
Quiver
Needlework

Gina Yates
Narcissus Nobody

MEMOIR & BIOGRAPHY

Nassrine Azimi and Michel Wasserman
Last Boat to Yokohama: The Life and Legacy of Beate Sirota Gordon

William S. Burroughs & Allen Ginsberg
Don't Hide the Madness: William S. Burroughs in Conversation with Allen Ginsberg edited by Steven Taylor

James Carr
BAD: The Autobiography of James Carr

Judy Gumbo
Yippie Girl

Judith Malina
Full Moon Stages: Personal Notes from 50 Years of The Living Theatre

Phil Marcade
Punk Avenue: Inside the New York City Underground, 1972–1982

Jililian Marshall
Japanthem: Music Connecting Cultures Across the Pacific

Alvin Orloff
Disasterama! Adventures in the Queer Underground 1977–1997

Nicca Ray
Ray by Ray: A Daughter's Take on the Legend of Nicholas Ray

Stephen Spotte
My Watery Self: Memoirs of a Marine Scientist

PHOTOGRAPHY-MEMOIR

Mike Watt
On & Off Bass

SHORT STORY ANTHOLOGIES

SINGLE AUTHOR

The Alien Archives: Stories
by Robert Silverberg

First-Person Singularities: Stories
by Robert Silverberg
with an introduction by John Scalzi

Tales from the Eternal Café: Stories
by Janet Hamill, with an introduction by Patti Smith

Time and Time Again: Sixteen Trips in Time
by Robert Silverberg

Voyagers: Twelve Journeys in Space and Time
by Robert Silverberg

MULTI-AUTHOR

Crime + Music: Twenty Stories of Music-Themed Noir
edited by Jim Fusilli

Dark City Lights: New York Stories
edited by Lawrence Block

The Faking of the President: Twenty Stories of White House Noir
edited by Peter Carlaftes

Florida Happens: Bouchercon 2018 Anthology
edited by Greg Herren

Have a NYC I, II & III: New York Short Stories;
edited by Peter Carlaftes & Kat Georges

Songs of My Selfie: An Anthology of Millennial Stories
edited by Constance Renfrow

The Obama Inheritance: 15 Stories of Conspiracy Noir
edited by Gary Phillips

This Way to the End Times: Classic and New Stories of the Apocalypse
edited by Robert Silverberg

MIXED MEDIA

John S. Paul
Sign Language: A Painter's Notebook (photography, poetry and prose)

DADA

Maintenant: A Journal of Contemporary Dada Writing & Art (Annual, since 2008)

HUMOR

Peter Carlaftes
A Year on Facebook

FILM & PLAYS

Israel Horovitz
My Old Lady: Complete Stage Play and Screenplay with an Essay on Adaptation

Peter Carlaftes
Triumph For Rent (3 Plays)
Teatrophy (3 More Plays)

Kat Georges
Three Somebodies: Plays about Notorious Dissidents

TRANSLATIONS

Thomas Bernhard
On Earth and in Hell
(poems of Thomas Bernhard with English translations by Peter Waugh)

Patrizia Gattaceca
Isula d'Anima / Soul Island
(poems by the author in Corsican with English translations)

César Vallejo | Gerard Malanga
Malanga Chasing Vallejo
(selected poems of César Vallejo with English translations and additional notes by Gerard Malanga)

George Wallace
EOS: Abductor of Men
(selected poems in Greek & English)

ESSAYS

Richard Katrovas
Raising Girls in Bohemia: Meditations of an American Father

Far Away From Close to Home
Vanessa Baden Kelly

Womentality: Thirteen Empowering Stories by Everyday Women Who Said Goodbye to the Workplace and Hello to Their Lives
edited by Erin Wildermuth

POETRY COLLECTIONS

Hala Alyan
Atrium

Peter Carlaftes
DrunkYard Dog
I Fold with the Hand I Was Dealt

Thomas Fucaloro
It Starts from the Belly and Blooms

Kat Georges
Our Lady of the Hunger

Robert Gibbons
Close to the Tree

Israel Horovitz
Heaven and Other Poems

David Lawton
Sharp Blue Stream

Jane LeCroy
Signature Play

Philip Meersman
This Is Belgian Chocolate

Jane Ormerod
Recreational Vehicles on Fire
Welcome to the Museum of Cattle

Lisa Panepinto
On This Borrowed Bike

George Wallace
Poppin' Johnny

Three Rooms Press | New York, NY | Current Catalog: www.threeroomspress.com
Three Rooms Press books are distributed by Publishers Group West: www.pgw.com

CPSIA information can be obtained
at www.ICGtesting.com
Printed in the USA
JSHW041907171221
21240JS00004B/7

9 781953 103130